# THE MASSACRE BALL

BRIAN AND MINA'S HOLIDAY HITS, BOOK 3

## KITTY THOMAS

BURLESQUE PRESS

# THE MASSACRE BALL

KITTY THOMAS

*Burlesque Press*

**The Massacre Ball**

**Brian and Mina's Holiday Hits, Book 3**

Copyright © 2023 by Kitty Thomas

Printed in the United States of America

ISBN 13: 978-1-960480-25-5

Wholesale orders can be placed through the author.

Published by Burlesque Press

Contact the author at kittythomas.com Please use the "licensing" link in the top menu bar.

# ACKNOWLEDGMENTS

In no particular order, thank you to the following people for their help in The Massacre Ball:

My silver circle angel patrons, Mickey Roland, and Lilith Teaspirit.
Robin @ gobookcoverdesign.com for the cover art.
Morgan for being my alpha reader.
And Lori for the graphic teasers.
And to my the readers who loved Brian enough to want to see him in more books.
Thank you!

# CHAPTER 1
# BRIAN

S ummer has just slipped into fall. The morning is finally crisp enough for my favorite black leather jacket. It's warm and comforting and carries so many fond memories. I've killed so many people wearing this jacket.

I sit in a nondescript black sedan, parked a few yards away from a cul de sac in a nice suburban neighborhood, sipping my black coffee. Ordinarily this car wouldn't exactly be considered nondescript; I look like an agent from the government. But in this Upper Middle Class Pretending To Be Rich neighborhood, there are at least twenty other cars that look just like mine.

In fact, I'm currently parked in a driveway that normally has the same make and model, so it's perfect. Like fate.

The occupants of the house are at work. I'm just within receiving distance from the listening devices I have planted in the two-story house that sits nestled in the middle of the cul de sac.

I turn up the volume on the wireless receiver when I hear Aidan's aunt start to scream at him again. I flinch, pushing back the flashback to my own childhood. This feels all too familiar.

I've been watching this bitch for two and a half months, waiting, deciding her fate. And she is testing the very limits of my patience.

After all my plans blew up on the Fourth of July, and Mina and I had to go in and kill everybody by hand like we were running a murder craft fair, Aidan was the sole survivor. The kid hasn't spoken a word about what happened no matter how many nice police officers with milk, cookies, and a fake smile ask. I will never acknowledge it to anybody, but I kind of like this kid. He's tough for a little guy.

His father wasn't even declared dead because we took care of those bodies.

He's simply *missing*. The police have their suspicions, of course, but no body, no crime. Plus, this isn't exactly a crackpot top team of brilliant detectives like you see on TV. They're just normal people, made bitter by how many jackasses the world contains and the limits and constraints on their crime solving budgets. More than half the time when they send evidence off to a forensics lab, the results come back inconclusive or don't match anything on file. And then what?

All those fingerprints and DNA samples and other sundry clues are only useful if the bad guy is in a database somewhere, and I'm not. Neither is Mina. In real life, law enforcement relies on the dumbness of the average criminal to get caught doing some petty Starter Crime and end up "in the system". Until such stupidity is committed, the authorities are usually shit out of luck. It's not magic.

Sure, things like facial recognition software and the fact that everybody's phone is a spy camera and listening device now can make things tricky, but not impossible if you know what you're doing. And I do. So I doubt the mysterious disappearance of Stryker will ever be more than an unclosed case file collecting dust in the back of some filing cabinet.

But I haven't been watching Aidan to make sure he doesn't talk. Even if he talked, the police still wouldn't be any better off than they started when it comes to leads. I mean, he's five. Come on. They are *grasping* at straws here.

No, I'm watching his fucking caretaker. Eliza Snow is his mother's sister and seems to suspect Aidan's dad killed her. And she is very bitter about this supposed fact. I'm about eighty-six percent sure he didn't, but it is true that without Stryker's unsavory dealings, the mother would probably still be alive. So in his own way, maybe he did kill her. But my money is on one of his enemies. It's always one of the enemies.

There are two ways to go as a career criminal. You either stay out of relationships altogether so nobody has leverage on you, or you build a family to make you look respectable, always knowing and accepting they may eventually become collateral damage. Actually, there is a third option: you put an impenetrable security detail on your loved ones. But no security detail is truly impenetrable, so realistically you're working with the first two options.

Getting attached to anyone your enemies can use against you is the cardinal sin, and it appears that Aidan's father may have committed it. Either way, this bitch has hit Aiden on three different occasions in the space of two months. Eliza Snow isn't the name you would associate with the evil stepmother of the story, she sounds more like the princess lost in the woods.

She resents being thrust into motherhood when that wasn't her life plan. And Aidan looks a bit too much like his father for her tastes. She has a high-powered career and no husband—otherwise known as... nobody who will miss her.

Mina doesn't even know I'm doing this—watching this house and this kid. I can't bring myself to tell her about it yet—or if all goes well, ever. It would kill the very last bit of evil reputation I have with her, and I just can't be her whipped puppy. I can't. I am a killer, and any time I do something soft and nice that makes me seem like something more, I know I'm only misleading her.

I will never be more than a monster, and while maybe she's grown darker, she'll never be as bad as me. I don't want to give her the false hope that we can ever have some fairy tale romance—some sweet happily ever after. I'm not that guy. I would say she knew that from the beginning, but it wasn't as though she chose me. I chose her, and she had to mold herself around that new reality. Whatever feelings she may have developed for me since then, no doubt started as Stockholm Syndrome. And is it even possible for a relationship started that way to end in anything real? I have my doubts.

I hear a noise I can't quite discern, and then Aidan is crying. I don't know if she hit him again or just threw something in his direction. I tense.

"Pull yourself together, you've got school," she hisses, her voice so inhuman it rivals mine. We'll see how she deals with a grown up version soon enough. I grit my teeth and wait.

Everything inside me wants to run into that house and choke the fucking life out of this bitch. She's too much like what made me this way, and she has no idea the fire she plays with by just existing on my radar.

I let out a slow breath when I hear the brakes creak on the school bus as it pulls into the cul de sac and stops, waiting for Aidan to come out so he can go to first grade. Normally they start them in first grade at six, but he'll be six next month. It's close enough. I don't want to think about why I know these random facts about elementary school all of a sudden.

Back on the Fourth of July while I was helping the cleaners, Mina and I exchanged some text messages, half-joking about adopting the kid and me going to PTA meetings. That may as well be reality for all I know now about Aidan's schedule and the life and times of an almost six year old.

"Go," Eliza says.

He practically runs out the door. I can see him now on the front stoop, wiping his eyes with the back of his hand. My jaw clenches. He looks sad and scared, but I recognize the anger that simmers underneath it all. He's so young to carry that anger, but it's there.

I know part of it is at me for killing his father. Fair. But Eliza has been filling his head with all sorts of ideas about how and why his mother may have died—all to justify her cruelty to the kid, the one innocent in all this. At this rate he won't be innocent for long. In a decade he'll be a teenager, and the first true indications of what he is will bubble to the surface amid shock from everyone—including those who made him that way.

I'm under no such illusions. I knew the moment I killed his father in front of him that someday he would be like me. I just wasn't expecting him to re-live my entire backstory.

This is why I wanted to just let him blow up in the building. It would have been better for everyone. But because I chose mercy—for Mina—this kid is now locked into an unstoppable chain of events. And his current situation just locks him onto this trajectory with more finality.

If I don't get rid of the aunt, he gets abused for years and turns out a monster. If I do get rid of her, it's another close family member dying in a brutal way, which will fuck him up more, even if he's not close to her.

There is a third option, reporting her to child protective services, but I already know they won't take the report seriously. Ms. Snow looks too squeaky clean on paper. She even has a golden retriever. And they don't want another case file. I do at least know he wouldn't go into foster care. Aidan has a lot of relatives, but the next in line is an Uncle Martin on his father's side, who may or may not fear Aidan rising to take the throne of his father's criminal empire. So is it safe to leave him with Uncle Martin? I guess we're about to find out.

And how many people will I have to kill so this kid has a semi-stable home environment? As though any home environment littered with a string of corpses could ever be stable. This kid is so beyond fucked.

Aidan climbs onto the bus, a little shaky, and moves to one of the seats at the very back. He slides into it by himself, and something tightens in my chest. The only other person who has ever made me feel this much is Mina.

I watch as the bus circles the cul de sac and drives past the house I'm parked at. His gaze shifts in my direction, and I turn quickly away. I don't need him to be a witness to two of my crimes.

I wait a few more minutes to get my emotions under control. I don't like this, going into a kill with *emotions*. It's not right. This is too personal to me, and when a kill is too personal, that's when you fuck it all up. But there is no possible way I can let this kid live in this house with this witch whose abuse will only escalate the longer I leave him here.

He's not going to stop looking like his father any time soon. In all likelihood he'll only grow to look more and more like him as the years pass. And the speed with which the abuse started... it too closely mirrors my own experience. I'm not leaving him to live out that story. There was no avenging angel to save me, but Aidan—even though he may not yet realize it—is quite a bit luckier.

I push down the thoughts of how my chosen actions will also negatively impact him. The aunt kept a distance from the family, but she is still his family. And unfortunately, she looks a bit like his mother. So if I kill her, am I killing his mother all over again—or the last remaining living connection to her?

Fuck.

I hate having to weigh this kind of shit. This is not normal. I never should have started keeping tabs on this kid. What I didn't know wouldn't hurt me. I should have just let his fate play out because it's clear, nothing I do is going to change it.

# CHAPTER 2

# BRIAN

I knock on the front door. A moment later it swings open. Eliza, obviously thinking Aidan missed his bus, seems ready to start shouting, but then she notices me.

"Oh," she says. "Hello." She says it with a bit of a question mark at the end.

I allow my gaze to drag slowly over her. She's far more attractive up close than brief glimpses during my surveillance allowed me to catalog. She'd fetch a good price at the house. But I shake that thought out of my head.

I would have to keep Eliza's identity a secret, and the one normal functional relationship quality I have with Mina is honesty. And if I did tell her, she'd never forgive me for ripping a non-kinky woman out of her normal life and into the darkness of the house. She's got a soft spot for the women.

Shame, because it's a great financial opportunity—not that I give much of a fuck about finances, but it seems like a somewhat normal thing to think about. And lately I've been trying to think more about what seems normal. I live in fear that one day Mina will wake up and think: *"Well. He really is an irredeemable sociopath."* and pull away from me for good.

But I mainly look at Eliza this way to get her to drop her guard.

I'm not unaware of my charms and that air of danger so many women are so attracted to. If she thinks I want to fuck her instead of murder her, it might get me in the door. After all, I've been watching this house for a while and despite her beauty, she doesn't have a lot of gentleman callers. I also happen to know—courtesy of the listening devices—that she goes through a lot of batteries.

"I hate to trouble you, but my phone died, and I was wondering if I could use yours." I put a bit of Gabe's *Aww Shucks Ma'am* drawl into my voice.

She hesitates. "Where's your car?"

I point up at the house across the way. She recognizes it. Or thinks she does.

"Oh! You must be my neighbor."

How oblivious can she be to only know her neighbors by their cars?

"Guilty," I say, plastering a sheepish grin onto my face. "I went off and locked my keys in the house. Donna is always saying I need to put my house key on the same ring as my car key," I say, shifting my cover from hapless sexy stranger to non-intimidating neighbor.

She looks a bit disappointed at the mention of a wife, but the guy in that house does have a wife named Donna, and surely Eliza has noticed her out gardening before. But the fact that I'm now her neighbor and have a wife bitching at me about how I organize my keys, drops her guard even further. And I don't need to seduce her, I just need inside the house.

She opens the door, "Please, come in."

I don't think I could be happier at those words if I were a vampire. I smile and cross the threshold into the foyer. The golden retriever growls at me and starts barking.

"Shut up, Baxter!" she snaps.

He whimpers and gets that sad dog face where you see too much of the whites of their eyes.

She turns around to dig through her purse, and I take the opportunity to grab her and slam her against the wall.

"You should have listened to your dog. He's got far better instincts than you do."

The dog barks again and leaps on me. I did *not* expect that from a golden retriever. I shake him off and grab the gun from the back of my pants. I shoot a nearby lamp, and the shattering glass sends the dog running out the still open front door. It would have been easier to shoot him, but Aidan loves that dog.

By this point, Eliza is running up the stairs—just like the dumb horror movie victim. I pull the gloves from my jacket pocket and slip them on.

All this dumb bitch had to do was not hurt the kid. All she had to do was give him a safe place to live and maybe just maybe he could grow up semi-normal, but the evil rot in her is the same as my stepmother's. There is no saving her, and only one way to get Aidan out of her care.

"I'm calling the police!" she says from behind the locked bedroom door when I bang on it.

"With what? A tin can and string?" She never got her phone out of her bag.

"I have a landline, you piece of shit!"

"No you don't."

She's dead quiet.

"H-how do you know that?"

"What difference does it make at this point?" I kick in the door.

"You're not my neighbor."

I laugh. "Wow, that's probably the most clearly obvious thing I've ever heard a person say out loud. Congratulations."

She grabs a lamp and swings it at me. She gets me in the shoulder, but I've already grabbed her and pushed her against the wall.

There is a part of me that knows deep down I don't have to do this. I can make a different choice. Surely the threat of me now is big enough that I could make sure she never raises a hand to Aidan again, but she'd call the police. I wouldn't be able to get close to the house again. They'd find my bugs. Too many things could go wrong.

Besides, it's too late now. When I look into her eyes I see my stepmother, and there is only one way that story ever ends.

"You don't have to do this. Do you want money? Take whatever you want. I don't care. It's all insured."

But I only barely hear the words, and their meanings certainly don't register in time for my rational sanity to come back online.

A moment later she's grabbed a cigarette out of a nearby ash tray and presses the burning ember against the side of my neck. And with that one small act, any chance of mercy is gone.

"Not this time, Linda," I say.

"Who's Linda?" They are the last words she says before my hand crushes her windpipe.

The body slides to the ground, and I give her lifeless corpse a kick and then back away. Who the fuck even smokes anymore? I look down to find my hands shaking. This never happens to me, well, not since the very first time. I squeeze my eyes shut and put my hands over my ears, blocking out Linda's shouts and the sound of the switch slicing through the air... my dog whimpering...

My ears ring, and the room gets very loud with a long tone before I readjust to the silence of the room. It's only then that I finally hear the dryer down the hallway. I jump at the sound of the dog barking again, but then he sees Eliza. He blinks and looks at the body and then looks at me and back at the body again.

He's thinking as hard as I've ever seen any dog think—as though he's trying to decide if she's worth mourning.

"She kicked you a couple of times, too," I say.

He just whimpers and slinks out of the room and back down the stairs as though he actually understood those words. I flush the cigarette butt down the toilet in the attached bathroom and follow the dog downstairs. I shut the front door so he can't get out again and put food and water in his dish.

He eyes me warily, but nothing can keep him from his food bowl for long. Then I go through the house and remove all the listening devices.

I'm still shaky when I get back out to the car, but I start it up and pull away. Once I'm well outside the neighborhood I use a burner phone to tip off the police about the murder then toss the phone out the window. I couldn't let Aidan come home to that. I just hope they find a delicate way to get him to his Uncle Martin's house. There's no reason he needs to go to another funeral right now.

When I get back to the house, I find Mina in our dungeon room, staring at the wall.

"What is this?" she asks. She hasn't yet noticed my clearly shattering mental state, and I'm glad for the brief reprieve.

"That's my murder wall. It's just something I'm trying."

There are photos and thumbtacks and post-its and red strings connecting things. I guess now is as good a time as any to tell her about the new contract.

# CHAPTER 3
# MINA

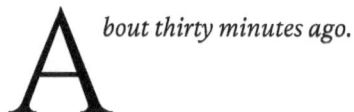

A*bout thirty minutes ago.*

WHEN I OPEN MY EYES, Brian is already gone. He's been already gone a lot lately. Something has been off since the ill-conceived plot to blow up the Stryker building during the Fourth of July parade. I've asked him where he goes a few times, and why we're not going together, but he brushes me off.

I don't want to be *that girl*, you know, the one who needs to know exactly what her boyfriend is doing at all times, but... if he's letting me in on his world and his side jobs, shouldn't I know about anything that pertains to that? I laugh out loud in the empty dungeon room, thinking about Brian as my *boyfriend*. He is so not my boyfriend.

Though he did get me those almost-black roses for our murder date. They lived a whole 3 weeks. I kept them upstairs in the gym, so they could get some light.

Things have been pretty quiet at the house lately. Most of the girls have been steering clear of Brian's wrath, there have been no good contracts the past couple of months, and no misbehaviors among the pleasure house's clientele.

So Brian has become increasingly antsy. I can feel it in him, this need to kill something. And I'd be lying if I said the beast curled up inside of me isn't making the same grumbling noises. I don't know if Brian's darkness feels like an itch under his skin, but it feels like one in mine.

The first time it happened, I tried moisturizing. Nope. It wasn't until Easter when I killed Matsumoto's son and a guard, that I realized this dark thing inside me was no longer content to just be *okay* with Brian killing. It wanted some of the action, too.

I feel like a cartoon character as I dramatically stretch and yawn. The side table says it's eleven o'clock. Great.

I hate it when Brian doesn't set the alarm. He's got this internal alarm that wakes him up like clockwork, and I have no idea how he does it without sunlight cues. Normally he wakes me, but when he's gone like this, I'm left to wake myself, which means I end up missing out on the house's breakfast buffet.

I sigh and swing my legs over the side of the bed, and that's when I look up.

What in the fuck?

Also, how did I sleep through this? Was Brian just in here in the middle of the night with a black light, setting all this up? I probably should see a sleep specialist to find out if this is normal.

I don't know how, but somehow, there is... I don't know what they're called. It's like... when you watch a show about a serial killer, and the police have this wall up and there are newspaper clippings, and photos, and thumbtacks holding stray sticky notes to the wall, and then red strings that connect things, and giant question marks trying to see if this thing links to that thing?

So yeah, that's what I'm looking at right now. There is a photo of an older gentleman in a suit in the middle of the board. He has thin wire-rimmed glasses and a very distinguished look about him. Above his photo is the name: Drake Windsor. There are a few index cards, thumb tacked to... wait, this is a stone wall, how does he have things thumbtacked?

I press my fingertips against it. Okay, so he's put in a whole cork board underneath this, and again, my question is how? Why? What is happening right now? So he's got these index cards with some facts about Drake Windsor who I assume is a new contract.

He's a widower, apparently. His children are grown and live out of state. Brian has noted here that "they won't be a problem". Well, that's reassuring.

There's a second photo on the board of a clearly Italian man that says Dante Valentino. And below that, another index card makes it clear that he's the guy who put out the hit on the guy that looks like a rich librarian.

There's a picture of a Jack-O-Lantern tacked in the bottom right corner, with a pink sticky note asking, "Halloween Masquerade Ball, get invite?" and another blue note that reads, "Six weeks enough time?" There's a red string that connects this note back to Dante's photo and another blue note that reads, "Wants job done soon. Will he wait this long?"

Before I can read more, I hear the door behind me open, and I know it's Brian, not just because nobody else is suicidal enough to enter our room uninvited—not that we're entertaining guests down here—but because I can feel his cold, empty energy, which somehow feels like a blanket of silence that wraps around me and makes me feel calm inside like the first snow of winter.

"What is this?" I ask, not turning around.

"That's my murder wall. It's just something I'm trying."

I just stand here with this thought for a moment and let it gel. There's this part of me that thinks it's completely cute that Brian made a murder wall and actually *calls it* his murder wall. I like it. It means I'm going to know what he knows when he knows it about jobs, and I won't have to follow him around like an annoying sidekick trying to get him to talk about things.

"How did it get here?"

"Elves," he deadpans. "What do you mean how did it get here? I set it up last night when I couldn't sleep."

I try to imagine Brian making a two a.m. run to the office supply store and then... doing all of this. But I just can't picture it—especially the Jack-o-Lantern. Did he clip it out of a magazine? Does he have a stash of Better Homes and Gardens hidden under our bed? Terrifying, if true.

"It's missing something," I say, still assessing the wall. "We should add some Washi tape."

"What the fuck is Washi tape?"

I turn then because I've finally noticed the edge in his voice. He looks a bit pale. "Brian? Are you all right?"

"Fine."

He is absolutely not fine, but I don't push him. I wonder if it's connected to where he's going when he slips off. I don't worry that he's cheating on me. Unless cheating means killing people without me—that's just not Brian. He's far more interested in killing people than he is fucking them. It's not like he's never fucked a woman down here in the dungeon, but it's just not like that. It's not romantic and hearts and kisses. It isn't even passion. I probably should be bothered, but I'm not. As he's said on many occasions, fucking from him is not a compliment. Even now, he doesn't trust himself to have real full-on sex with me unless he's tied up for the event, which I'm happy to accommodate.

I don't know what he imagines would happen or how it could go south, but he's adamant about this.

The only mistress I have to worry about is Death—as in the general principle. Probably not my own—at least not at Brian's hands.

He closes his eyes when I press a hand against the side of his face and lean in to press a soft kiss to his lips.

He returns the kiss then pulls away and sighs. "I killed someone this morning," he confesses.

"Without me?"

"It wasn't like that. It was just something I had to do and it... it brought up some things."

Childhood things. He doesn't have to say it. The specter of his stepmother hangs over him even after all these years. Even killing her and burying the pieces in multiple states couldn't stop her relentless pursuit of him in flashbacks and nightmares.

He says it's not as bad since he's had me, but sometimes it's pretty bad.

"Soooo," I say, pulling his attention back to the here and now. "New contract?"

He nods. "New contract."

"I better get to go."

He smirks. "Or what?" The haunted look in his eyes has faded away, replaced with the wicked gleam reserved only for me.

"I do get to go, right?"

He chuckles. "Yes, you get to go."

"On Halloween?"

"If I can swing it, that's when I thought we could take him out. Windsor is a paranoid man and always heavily guarded, but at a party where he's relaxed with everyone around him singing his praises, we should be able to find our moment."

"But... Halloween. It's so far away."

He arches a brow. "Relax, Killer. I've got another side job we can go on together." He pulls a folded up piece of paper from his pocket and waves it in the air, teasing me.

"Another contract?"

"Nope. Anton stopped me upstairs, and apparently one of our buyers doesn't understand the consequences of breaking house rules."

"Oh, let me kill him. You already got to kill someone today." And besides, the men who break house rules are abusing the women they bought, so I definitely want to be the one to spill blood.

Brian just smirks.

## CHAPTER 4
# BRIAN

"What do you think?"

I turn to find Mina in a black corset and black leather pants with matching boots. "What am I supposed to be commentating on?" I ask, confused. This is pretty much the standard attire she's worn every time we've been in a killing people situation together. That's only been a few times, but still, a pattern is emerging.

"This corset. Do you think it's too tight?"

"Are you planning to seduce him before you kill him?" I ask, waggling my eyebrows as I zero in on her cleavage.

"Hilarious. I mean... I don't know if I can move properly in this one."

"You seem to be moving fine to me. You look great, Killer. Now let's go."

She blushes, but follows me out to the car.

"Why are you so jumpy?" I ask.

"Do we have everything?"

"I always keep this car ready to go for standard house jobs."

She nods, and puts her seatbelt on. "But do I have a bag? With *my* guns?"

"Yes, you've got a bag." I pull the car through the circular driveway and out onto the main road. "What's this about, Mina?"

"I don't know. It's just... at Easter I didn't think about it, I just came to get you. And then for the Fourth of July there was a lot of planning, and it was going to be a boring button push anyway..."

"Famous last words."

She laughs a little, but continues, "I don't know, we didn't plan for this. What if something happens?"

I squeeze her knee. "Nothing's going to happen. These guys aren't hardened criminals. They're idiots with a kink, and some of them break our rules. So we enforce."

"What's going to happen to the girl?"

I'm quiet, keeping my eyes on the road.

"Brian?" she prods.

I sigh. "I don't know, Mina. It depends."

"Like fuck it does. She's coming back with us. Promise me."

"We can't run a halfway house for damaged toys."

"Promise me."

My jaw clenches, but I say, "Fine."

We have clients all over the world, but this is a local so it takes less than an hour to get there.

Despite this guy's wealth, his security is well below the standard it should be. Contrary to expectation, not everybody with money fully understands how much they have to lose, or how easy it is to take it.

So we just roll in past a gate that isn't even locked with a camera that isn't even on. Fucking amateurs. I can tell Mina's still nervous as we pull up.

"I still can't believe you just... *show up*."

"It depends on the people involved. There are exceptions where I have to plan, like when I came for you in Japan. But this guy? He's nothing."

She nods finally and gets out of the car. We strap ourselves down with the weapons in our bags then go up and ring the bell.

A refined older gentleman opens the door. A butler.

Mina shakes her head at me. Did she know I was planning to snap his neck, or just that I intended to kill him? I give her a reassuring look then pull my gun. The man's eyes widen.

"Oh, don't look so shocked. You know you're employer isn't a boy scout. Tell me how many people are in the house right now."

"J-just Mr. Dinmore."

"What about the girl?" Mina says.

"I'm afraid I don't know what you mean, Miss."

Mina pulls her own gun and trains it on the butler. "Tell me about the girl, Jeeves, or I'll kill you myself."

"I-I-I..."

*Now* he can't get control of his vocabulary?

"The truth!" she barks.

He jumps at her tone, and the stress of two guns on him. "I... she... he... I don't know. She... she's not here."

"*Where* is she?" Mina presses.

Finally he caves and the truth comes out in a rush. "I-in the garden. B-buried in the garden. It was an accident!"

A moment later the butler's brains are on the wall.

"Oh, so you get to kill the butler?"

"He's not an innocent," she snarls back at me.

Well, okay then. I follow her in her rampage down the house's long hallway. We finally find Dinmore cowering under his own desk in his study. I see his shadow under the desk and tilt my head at Mina. She nods and jumps up on the desk like a cat.

"I-I've got a gun," he says.

Stupid fucking thing to say. If you've got it, shoot it. I aim my 9mm at the flat wooden panel of the desk and unload the magazine. The bullets go straight through and hit their target. I watch as a pool of blood spreads out under the desk.

"I was going to do it!" Mina shouts.

"Too risky. He had a weapon. I wasn't going to risk him pulling that same trick on you."

She leans over the desk to peer underneath at the man.

"He doesn't even have a gun, Brian. He was bluffing. Dammit!"

"You got to shoot the Butler."

"It's not the same."

"Let's bury them in the garden with the girl," I suggest.

She sighs. "Okay."

The cafeteria is full when we arrive back at the house. They still aren't used to seeing Mina like this, and it pisses me off the way some of the other girls act around her now. Jealous. *They* chose to come here to be trained for the highest bidder. None of us ripped them out of their beds in the middle of the night.

It's not Mina's fault if some of them decided a bit too late that maybe they should have stayed in college and stayed in control of their own lives instead of turning a sexual fantasy into their entire personality.

In the hush that falls over the room, the voice of one of the newer girls drifts to my ears. "Look at her. Mina thinks she's the shit. I'd love to see Brian truly punish her to wipe that smirk off her face."

There are a few gasps, and I can just make out Annette's voice to my right. "Oh shit, she didn't just say that." Always the concerned house mother.

I can feel my entire face going cold and dark as I slowly turn toward the offending new girl. But before I can move, Mina breezes past me, the click-clack of her high-heeled boots deafening in the now silent room. I watch as she grabs the girl by the front of her shirt and hauls her to stand.

"Fiona, you're still pretty new." Her words come out crisp and sharp, the way she was with Matsumoto at Easter. "I'm going to give you a chance to apologize before I have to make an example of you in front of everyone."

Fiona rolls her eyes. "Whatever, Bitch."

I start in the direction of Fiona when Mina hauls back and smacks the girl hard across the face, leaving a bright red handprint, and then I realize what's happening. She's protecting this girl from me. She's handling it, so I won't.

I hang back and observe, curious. Everyone in the cafeteria has been stunned into silence by this display.

"I can do whatever I want to you right now and nobody here will stop me," Mina says, staring her down.

I glance over to find Gabe watching me for my response to this show.

Fiona remains defiant for only a few more seconds before she shrinks back and mumbles, "I-I'm Sorry."

"I'm sorry, what?" Mina, hisses.

"I-I'm sorry, Ma'am."

"Good. That was your only warning. You're on my radar, dear. And that's a bad place to be."

Fiona seems to melt back into her chair as Mina takes a good long look around the room. Her eyes finally meet mine, and I raise a brow at her. I see the smallest shrug of her shoulder before she turns to join Annette and another new girl at their table.

Was Mina protecting that girl, or was she protecting my reputation? I don't even know anymore. Gabe moves closer to me and speaks low so that only I can hear him.

"Do you remember Dmitri Barinov?"

"That slimy bastard Anton wanted us to partner up with?" I ask. I thought we were doing just fine on our own and didn't need to be bringing any new blood into things. Barinov is too similar to Stryker for my tastes.

"One and the same," Gabe says. "And, do you remember Julie?"

I raise a brow. "I'm not sure what you think is wrong with my memory, but yeah... that girl you moped over for months? Pretty sure I remember."

He points at the table Mina is sitting at. She seems to be involved in a discussion with the famous Julie. "I found her in Dmitri's establishment. I want that motherfucker and all his men dead. Do you think you and Mina can handle it?"

"Not for free. I only do jobs specifically for the house, unless it's a contract."

"Since when did you care about the money?"

I shrug. "I'm not your pit bull, Gabe."

"How much?"

"I'll do it for a couple million."

"What? That's insane!"

"That's me and my girl's going rate, now. Take it or leave it."

"Fine. I'll take it."

"Mina!" I shout across the cafeteria.

She turns to look at me, all demure. "Yes, Master?"

I have to fight the eye roll. Do people in this house really buy this anymore? I glance around the room. Clearly they do. I guess the reality of our actual relationship would be too surreal for them to consider. I motion for her to join us and then we go with Gabe to iron out the details.

# CHAPTER 5
## MINA

I let out a low whistle when Brian steps out of the bathroom, Friday night. My brain is barely able to comprehend what I'm seeing. Brian, in a suit.

Brian. In a suit.

"Mina? Are you okay?"

I shake my head. "I am not okay. You're wearing a suit. You look so... suave."

He smirks.

"Like James Bond," I add helpfully.

"You could have stopped at suave."

Fair enough.

"Where are you going?" I don't know if I want to let him out of the house looking like this. I mean I know his energy doesn't exactly invite a lot of women to cozy up to him, but still.

"Where are *we* going," he corrects.

"Where are *we* going?" I ask, playing along, but on the inside, I'm excited. And more importantly, what am I wearing?

He answers both my spoken and unspoken question by laying a black garment bag across the bed and handing me a thick cream-colored invitation on Crane stationery.

"I scored this invite to the Windsor Estate tonight."

I goggle at the envelope in my hand. "I thought you said the job wasn't until Halloween. That's still almost six weeks away. We're not ready."

"It is on Halloween. This is just a cocktail party. Just a little reconnaissance."

I unzip the garment bag to find a black floor length evening gown. He glances down at the Longines watch he liberated from the Stryker building back in July. Though it isn't cheap, it's certainly nothing close to a high-end luxury watch, and Brian doesn't generally care much about that anyway. I'm sure he's only wearing it because it's a trophy from our last kills.

"We don't have a lot of time," he says, "Party starts in an hour."

*Thanks for the notice, Brian.*

I pull the invitation from the envelope and scan it. "So how did you get invited to this again?"

"The same way I'm on the guest list for the Halloween Masquerade Ball."

I'm actually not completely sure how that happened, either.

Off my expression, he says, "I know Drake Windsor."

I stare at Brian, waiting for a punch line that never arrives. He *knows* the target?

"If you know him already, why do you need the murder wall?" I wave an arm dramatically at the wall in question.

"Distance. It's more dangerous to take a job where you know the target. Too easy to get sloppy and leave a trail. But there are five other contract killers who've been invited to tonight's party, so when it does happen, suspicions will be spread out."

"How do you know him?" I ask, skimming right past the fact that this Windsor guy seems to be cozy with at least six contract killers.

Brian arches a brow and points at the dress I'm still half staring at. I begin to strip out of my Queen of the Damned uniform and get into the evening gown.

"Happy?" I ask, once dressed.

His gaze sweeps over my body in that predatory way that still sends a shiver down my spine.

"Very." He rotates his finger in the air. "Turn."

I turn and pull my hair up for him to zip the dress. His tongue trails up my back just ahead of the zipper, then he slides a hand between my legs, and I open for him. If I had any doubts before, I have none now about why this dress has such a high side slit.

"Take off your panties," he growls in my ear.

"W-why? We're going to be late."

He smacks my ass with his other hand. "You're being such a bad girl right now."

"Brian..."

"Because I want easy access at the party tonight."

His words send a bolt of desire through me even more potent than what his hand between my thighs commands.

"How do you know Drake?" I ask again, leaning back against him. He presses open mouthed kisses over my throat, playing at the edges of my collar that most people outside the house believe to be just a nice piece of jewelry. The platinum filigree choker, inlaid with onyx stones to match my grandmother's ring really does go with everything.

"I've done a few jobs for him in the past," Brian says.

I pull back and spin around to face him. "What?!?"

"How else would he know so many professionals?" He says this as though the only profession in the world is murder for hire.

"So now you all are fighting to be the one to kill him?"

Brian shrugs. "It's just business."

I think there's more to it, but I let it go.

"Is it an open contract?" I ask as I go to our closet and slip into a pair of black heels.

"I'm assured I'm the only one who's been asked, but I'm not sure I trust the guy."

"If you don't trust the guy, then why are you taking the job?"

Brian shrugs, and I know he has no plans to say anymore about this right now.

It's after dark when we arrive at the Windsor Estate. The heavily guarded iron gate extends around Drake Windsor's massive property which seems to go on for miles. I grip Brian's arm and lean in to whisper in his ear as we walk along the well-lit path up to the front door.

"What about weapons?" I whisper.

"No weapons," he says. "They'll pat us down and send us all through a metal detector inside."

"Then how in the fuck are we going to do this? Are you planning to kill him with your bare hands?"

Brian shrugs. "I could. He's too refined to get his own hands dirty. He's old money."

"What does he do? Besides hiring assassins to kill all his enemies." You'd think Brian would have listed this man's profession on the murder wall.

"Oil magnate."

"Is that even still a thing?"

"Apparently," he says.

"I thought you'd tell me he was in the tech industry."

Brian laughs. "I said *old* money."

"Fossil fuel. Checks out." Dinosaurs are for sure old.

I stop talking as we get closer to the house. It's so big, even the word *mansion* doesn't quite cover it. The security detail are all big burly guys wearing suits and electronic ear pieces. They give us both a once over, their eyes staying on me a bit longer than is actually necessary.

The first one pats Brian down, and then goes for me, but Brian closes a tight grip over the man's wrist.

His voice is low and calm when he speaks. "Elvin, I swear to every power living and dead that if you touch her, you will not survive to see your daughter's first Christmas."

The guard swallows hard. "I have orders..."

"You have metal detectors. You and I both know that's the real security. This pat down business is just security theater—a display of Windsor's power and nothing more. You think about whether it's worth your life to participate in this charade."

He nods. "Go on in, Mr. Sloan." Then he nods at me, "Ma'am."

I can tell he's disappointed he won't get to pat me down. I just smile at him as we pass. But I let out a shuddering sigh of relief once we're to the second stage of security. I don't know if Brian knows this, but I'm pretty sure a guy like that touching me in any way as intimate as a pat down would have sent me spiraling into flashbacks from my past, which is the last thing I need tonight.

The fact that Windsor manhandles all his party guests like this adds a mark against him and explains why someone might want to hire someone to remove him from the gene pool.

Brian helps me get the platinum collar off and put it in the bin for jewelry next to the metal detectors. Windsor doesn't just have guards with discreet wands, he has full on metal detectors, like what you walk through at the airport.

I wonder if he gets a thrill out of making all his wealthy friends and acquaintances remove jewelry and cuff links to pass through his security—just a little humiliation ritual to make sure everyone knows who is top dog here. Brian removes a belt and his own cuff links. I didn't even know he *had* cuff links. He's clearly committed to playing the role of someone who belongs in this environment down to even the most non-essential trappings.

I stare up at the ornate vaulted ceilings. It does look a bit like a fancy airport in the entry hall. Once we get through security and put all our metal-containing finery back on, we have to pass through a second set of large walnut doors to get inside the main house and party.

White-gloved men in white tuxedos stand at this second set of doors. They nod at us and open them. I already hate this pompous Windsor guy. The display of opulence is disgusting.

"I thought wealth whispered," I say to Brian as we pass into the ballroom.

"Not at home, just in front of the peasants."

Well, *that* message has been delivered clearly. Brian leads me to an area away from the clusters of guests where we have some privacy.

"Why would he have two big parties so close together?" I'm sure it must annoy Brian that I have so many questions in a place where we should be keeping a low profile, but I'm just so curious. This is a pretty fancy party. Why does this guy *also* need to throw a masquerade ball on Halloween in six weeks? How often does he entertain?

Brian leans in close to my ear, one of his hands pressing lightly against my lower back when he does so. It takes a lot of concentration to hear his words over the loud rushing in my ears at the way my body reacts to these small touches. You'd think that after a while I would just somehow get used to Brian's intense energy, but I never do. When all his focus and attention is on me like this, it does things to me.

"The masquerade ball is a charity event he holds every year. Tickets are through the roof but there are are a lot of aspirational wealth social climbers that aren't part of his inner circle. Everyone here tonight is."

"Except for us and the others like us," I whisper back.

"I have my suspicions about that."

As if on cue, an older man in a sharp suit that broadcasts wealth approaches us. Even if I hadn't seen his photo on the murder wall, I'd know this is our target. He carries himself with too much confidence and just a dash of refined swagger. He knows he's the king here, and he knows everybody else knows it too.

He claps Brian on the back. "Sloan! I wasn't sure you'd accept my invitation."

"It seemed like a good excuse to impress my lady friend," Brian says.

Windsor turns to me, his gaze lingering longer than it should, and I can tell just by the look he gives me, that he thinks I've been hired for the night to be on Brian's arm. I refuse to let it offend me. If this guy knows Brian well at all, the idea that he might actually have a love interest is far too extreme a leap for most. Brian isn't exactly a big marshmallow.

Brian clears his throat, and Drake's lecherous gaze shifts, then he's all business again, dismissing me and going back to Brian. I hope Brian lets me kill this one.

"I've got to give a speech here in just a moment, but as soon as I'm done, I'd like to speak to you in my study about some business." He gives Brian a meaningful look as though they are speaking in some sort of secret code and of course as *the lady of the night* on Brian's arm, it's above my pay grade. If only this motherfucker knew.

"Of course," Brian says, with a tight smile.

Windsor excuses himself and winds through the crowd to get to the stage. As he starts his boring self-important soliloquy, I'm rescued from having to pay attention by the trays of champagne and *hors d' oeuvres* winding my way. I take a glass of champagne off a tray and one of the stuffed mushrooms off the other. Brian shakes his head at me when I offer him one.

When the trays pass by and we're alone again, he says, "I don't eat avant garde tiny food."

"Why not?"

"Because it's pretentious bullshit, and I don't do pretentious bullshit. Food like this is a way for smug rich assholes to signal their wealth and old money because nobody who just fell into money would wake up one morning and say, 'Today I think I'll have some fish eggs and snails.' Meanwhile all these other assholes are rambling on about their 'sophisticated palate.' More like sophisticated bullshit."

"But we need to blend in."

"Fuck that."

"Okay, so no on the stuffed mushrooms?"

"Definitely no."

"You never told me why you took this job." I wonder if there's some kind of personal vendetta between these two or if it's just another kill to him.

"Isn't this enough?" he says, gesturing. And I know he means the entire obnoxious show and all the pretension surrounding us.

"Your logic is sound," I say, popping the obnoxious, though admittedly delicious tiny food into my mouth.

"My logic is impeccable."

"Brian, is that really the only reason?"

"The money was good. Normally I don't shit where I eat but..."

"Tiny food?"

"Tiny food."

Windsor finally finishes his speech, gives a meaningful look to Brian and then exits off the stage.

"Well, that's my cue. Be good while I'm gone."

"I'll do my very best," I say as he leaves a lingering kiss against my neck.

# CHAPTER 6
# BRIAN

I follow Windsor away from the party to the private part of the house and up to his study on the second floor. He unlocks the door, flips on the light switch, and ushers me inside. I wish I could just kill him right here, right now, but it's far too messy.

Even though I've been to the Windsor Estate a few times before —enough to have the basic schematics down and know about some of the security he has in place—I don't know enough to pull a job here. The risk of getting caught is still too high. And Mina doesn't know to get out. I can't risk her being detained if things go wrong.

Besides, this is a golden opportunity to be inside the belly of the beast with new eyes.

I scan the room, pretending to be interested in the books on his bookshelves and the paintings on his walls. He's got The Count of Monte Cristo and Machiavelli's The Prince on his bookshelf. These choices don't surprise me. I'm not sure what exactly I'm looking for, but if there's anything in this room I need to know about, now would be the ideal time to collect it.

"That's a nice piece of ass you brought with you tonight," he says by way of introduction.

I keep my face blank and shrug. "She's okay on short notice. The agency assured me she was discreet at least." I know this fuckface thinks she's an escort, so may as well play into his assumptions. I'd rather he think she's a paid companion than to think she might be some kind of threat to him—or leverage he can use against me. I'd rather everyone underestimate her. And I'd like for him to underestimate me—not a small challenge given our work history together.

There's a buzzing sound and Windsor extracts a cell phone from his pocket. "Yes," he says, holding a finger up to me. Taking a call in the middle of important enough business to leave his swanky party is just one more signal that he considers me *the help* and barely worthy of the level of etiquette he would offer others of his station in life.

I watch as he goes behind his computer and types a few things in, pulls up something I can't see, then takes a thick white note card out of his desk's middle drawer along with a Montblanc fountain pen, but not just any Montblanc. I hate that I know this fact, but I do happen to know that this pen cost him two hundred and fifty-six thousand dollars. I vow right here and now that I will take that pretentious-as-fuck fountain pen as a trophy when I'm done.

He ends the call and looks up at me with what I'm sure is a mere mask of apology and not actual contrition. "I do apologize, but I have to deliver this to someone down at the party. I shouldn't be long. Please, make yourself comfortable and pour yourself a drink."

He rushes out the door. I glance over at the top shelf brandy in the decanter. But I'm not tempted. For all I know, someone tipped him off that I'd been hired to kill him, and he's beating me to the punch. Poison is typically a woman's method of choice, but we both know Windsor couldn't take me in a straight forward confrontation. I pour a glass anyway and place it on the outer part of the desk near one of the guest chairs.

Then I open the door to check down the hall. He is well and truly gone. I already checked for cameras. He's got one in the hallway just outside the door, but nothing within this room to monitor someone he's already invited inside. I assume this lack of surveillance is also for his own protection, so he can be free to do whatever seedy bullshit he needs to do within the confines of this room without leaving a record of it.

I slip on a pair of gloves, wipe down the doorknob I just touched, and take a look at his computer.

I don't know what I'm even looking for or what might be useful to know in this situation. I hadn't planned to be granted entrance into his inner sanctum. It's a rare stroke of luck, so of course, I don't trust it. I click through a few files and look at his browser history, then I immediately close out of everything.

I take a long slow breath. My hands are shaking and hot as I rip the gloves off and stuff them back into my inner jacket pocket. What the hell is wrong with me right now? I am so off my game. Ever since that fucking kid.

I pick up the brandy off the desk and go stare out the window trying to gather myself. I'm so tempted to risk poison just to have that shot of burning fire to calm my nerves.

There aren't a lot of things that bother me, but someone who hurts kids does. It doesn't matter the type of abuse, it's the fact that kids are helpless and innocent. I was helpless and innocent. Aidan is helpless and innocent. Anyone who would prey upon a child is a far worse monster than I'll ever be, and Windsor's computer is filled with evidence that he's that kind of monster.

Yes, I would have let Aidan blow up in that building, but it would have been a mercy killing. Not abuse. Not trauma. Not the things that steal your life from you and leave you either a terrified hollow shell forever, or empty of all conscience.

The door opens a few minutes later. "Oh, good, you're still here. I'm so sorry for that interruption."

"Not a problem." I work to conceal my rage and utter contempt for this piece of garbage. I was already going to kill him, but I didn't have any particular feelings about it before. It was just business.

"I'm so glad you accepted my invitation tonight. I have a job for you."

"Oh?" Of course the great and powerful Drake Windsor would

never sully himself by inviting me to such a lush affair of his equals if it wasn't because he needed me to kill someone.

"Dante Valentino. Do you know him?"

I keep my face blank of all expression. "Who doesn't?" I say. Dante is the man who hired me to kill Windsor. I wonder if he knows that already. Maybe he suspects and wants to kill Dante before Dante kills him.

"I know it's gauche to kill within your own circle," he says, "which is why the contract is so high. I'll pay you five million."

The silence stretches between us forever. Dante only offered me two for Windsor. And if this arrogant motherfucker hadn't left me alone in his study, I might be tempted to change the target. Before this moment I could have cared less whether it was Dante or Drake Windsor taking their last breaths under my watch.

I let out a low whistle as if I'm impressed by this kind of money. I mean in the grand scheme of things, he paid a quarter of a million dollars for a writing instrument, so by normal people pen buying standards, he's basically offering me the equivalent of a hundred dollars to take care of his problem.

I'm a little insulted.

"He must have done something to really piss you off."

"You could say that."

Putting out a hit on him would probably do it, though I still have no way to know he knows there's a hit out on him. It's not as though he'll volunteer that information.

"When do you need it done by?"

He lets out a sigh. "As soon as possible, but that's not very realistic, is it? You know Dante is always surrounded by heavy guard. He's a hard man to get to."

*Just like you.*

I nod and swirl my brandy around as though I've been savoring it this whole time.

"Did you plan to come to the Masquerade Ball on Halloween?" Windsor asks.

"I haven't decided yet."

"You could bring the piece of ass with you."

It takes all my self-control not to explode. I'm pretty certain he's just playing a role now. His tastes run a lot younger.

"I could," I say noncommittally.

"I'm inviting Dante. You could do it here."

"It's a lot of people. It's pretty risky. A lot could go wrong. I'd need hazard pay."

"What if I raise it to seven and I'll let you stash weapons in my house ahead of time and turn off the security cameras? I'll make sure my guards are all at the party and no one's in the video surveillance room."

"And I'm supposed to take that on a word and a handshake?"

"You can check it all out yourself. If it doesn't meet your standards, you can postpone the kill. It's a masquerade ball, so you'll already be wearing a mask, and all the men will be dressed the same. Black tuxedos. Not a lot of variation there. It's perfect cover."

Yes, I'd thought pretty much the same thing. It doesn't sit right with me that my target is now planning the kill of my employer a bit too closely to my own plans. I'm still not sure how much he knows or if he just suspects.

"Nine," I say.

"Done."

This guy? No, he doesn't know about the contract. Maybe he suspects Dante is moving in that direction, but I'd bet he doesn't know it's already active and that it's me. Drake Windsor doesn't have the balls to invite his killer into his private study with a counter offer. That's actually more Dante's style.

"I assume this isn't an open contract," I say, keeping my tone neutral.

"Oh, God no! Could you imagine the scandal?"

"Then why did you invite five of my colleagues to this party? It's really not your crowd."

"Backups, in case you said no."

"The money's good enough, and you know I don't have many scruples."

"It's what I love about you, Brian."

"Then you've got yourself a killer." I raise the glass of brandy and take the risk. This little bitch doesn't have the balls to poison me.

When I get back to the party, I find Mina standing near a window, a concerned look on her face. I guess I did take longer than intended. I move in behind her and press a kiss against the side of her neck.

"Miss me?" Before she can turn or reply, I take her hand and lead her off through the crowd. I'd originally intended to take her somewhere where I could do filthy things to her and use that as cover to glean more information about Windsor's security setup, but that won't be necessary now.

"Where are we going?" she asks, surprised when I lead her toward the front door.

"Home."

# CHAPTER 7
# BRIAN

I t's the first week of October, and once again I've slipped out of the house while Mina sleeps. That woman could sleep through a hurricane. I'm sitting across the street and a couple of houses down from the famous Uncle Martin. I was right that he was the next on the list to send the kid to. I don't know why he wasn't the first. I guess Eliza just looked better on paper. People always assume all women are maternal, and sometimes a kid pays for that miscalculation.

I should know.

It's a rich but not flamboyantly rich neighborhood. Stryker's businesses, both legitimate and less so are very successful, and Martin was a part of that success. He was supposed to be at that meeting on the Fourth of July, but he'd gotten hold of some bad tuna and apparently spent the entirety of the night in the bathroom instead. I heard rumors when I was skulking around at Stryker's memorial.

Officially Stryker is just missing—along with all the other men that were at the meeting that night—but they know. They know that many people don't just randomly wander off to go find themselves. There's talk that Martin was the one who killed everyone—or hired the hit at least. He wasn't. He really did eat bad tuna. He's the luckiest motherfucker in the world because if he'd been in that building that night, Aidan would be with the next guardian on the list right now.

Martin has taken over as CEO of Stryker, Inc. He's the top boss of both the front business and the back business, but there's whispering that legal provisions were made for Aidan to take over when he comes of age.

Martin's house is surrounded by several other houses, each a polite-enough distance apart. Each house has both a generous front and backyard.

The front door opens, and I shrink down in my seat when the kid comes out with the golden retriever.

I know this obsession I've developed isn't healthy.

My window is cracked so I hear when he says, "Good job, Baxter!"

The dog wags his tail as if a small child's approval of his pooping habits is the best thing that's ever happened to him. And then they go back inside.

It makes me uneasy having listening devices inside this house. His Uncle Martin is a career criminal. I worry they'll do a sweep of the house at some point and find what I've planted. I'm just making sure the kid is okay, and that my lack of self-control with Eliza doesn't land him in a worse situation.

I thought it was a good sign when Martin let the kid keep the dog. So far I haven't heard any signs of abuse. If he considers Aidan a threat to his criminal empire, he doesn't let it show. But Martin is getting on up in years, so maybe he plans to retire and hand the family business over to the kid. I guess we'll find out.

I jump when the burner phone on my dash rings.

"Talk," I say, not even glancing at the number. Only a couple of people have the number to this burner, and I'm not one for pleasantries and small talk.

"Is it done, yet?"

I sigh and roll my eyes. I swear working for this motherfucker isn't worth two million dollars. "Not yet, Dante. He's always under heavy guard. Halloween night at the Masquerade Ball is the best time. I've told you this."

"If you don't want the job, I can give it to someone else," he says.

"For your sake, I'm going to pretend you didn't say that. It'll be done Halloween night."

I disconnect the call before he can say anything else. Less than a minute later, the phone rings again.

"What!" I bark.

"Umm, Brian, I-I'm sorry. Is this a bad time?"

Windsor. The target, helping to plan his own murder. I plaster on a fake smile because I once heard you can hear a smile over the phone. I'm not sure if I believe that, but I'll use whatever techniques are available to appear more human when necessary.

"Not at all," I say. "What do you need?"

"Well," he hesitates a moment, and I grit my teeth, forcing myself not to snap at him. The last thing I want to do is spook the horse. "I was just thinking... I have a conservatory about a few acres back from the house. You could use that space."

"Conservatory like a greenhouse?" I ask.

I think he just nodded because I don't hear a reply, then finally, as though realizing he'd nodding at me through the phone, he says, "Y-yes, Kind of. It's not entirely glassed in, only one half of it. I thought the other side could be cleared out for your use."

"And how exactly will I lure Dante to the greenhouse?"

"I haven't thought of that part, yet. It's just a quiet space where no one will see or hear anything."

"Is that all?" I ask.

"For now. If there's any other way I can be of assistance, please don't hesitate to reach out."

"Will do," I say and disconnect the call.

So far he's called me on three different occasions making suggestions on weapons, body disposal, where I can hide things in his house, and how security will be diverted... I almost feel bad for the guy.

Almost.

# CHAPTER 8
# MINA

Halloween Night, The Masquerade Ball at the Windsor Estate.

"Don't be nervous," Brian whispers in my ear. But I can't help it. In a strange way this still feels like the first real job I've gone on with Brian, and I can't get past the idea that this seems all too easy, all too perfect.

"I'm fine," I say, forcing a smile. We've been at the party for an hour and I can't shake the feeling that this will all go terribly wrong somehow.

Once the target started planning his own murder with us, the murder wall just became a checklist of things that had been prepared or conveniently set up for us. Cameras off. Check. Weapons planted at various points around the house. Check. Kill room ready. Check—it's the conservatory a little way off from the main house. The plan for getting our target to that spot... well, since the real target is still Windsor, that part is different, but still. Our path has been made far too smooth for us, and I'm waiting for some kind of double cross—some big Halloween jump scare.

Tonight Brian is wearing a tuxedo, like all the other men, along with a black masquerade mask. The women all wear a mix of black and white evening gowns with masks to match. I'm wearing the same dress I wore for the cocktail party because Brian insisted. He says that side slit is too convenient, and he didn't get the opportunity to take advantage of it at the last party.

I'm sure he won't get the opportunity tonight, either, because I can't shake my nerves, and the last thing I'm thinking about right now is orgasms.

Drake Windsor hasn't been unguarded or alone the entire evening, and I'm not sure we're going to get our chance tonight. He's constantly surrounded with friends and guards. How do we have weapons conveniently stashed in the target's house, but can't even get him alone to use them?

Brian leans in close to my ear. "Will you be okay if I leave you for a while? I want to take a look around, see if I can figure out a way to lure him away. Keep an eye on him for me."

Brian has a syringe on him that he plans to inject Windsor with, so we can move him to the original planned kill location. He's got clothes planted for us so I can wear my normal clothes and not have to maneuver in a dress, and so he can look like part of the help. There's a large rolling cart with a sturdy bottom metal shelf and a floor-length white tablecloth over it to get the unconscious Windsor to our second location, but Brian has to get him alone and unconscious first.

I nod, even though I want to say no. But the last thing I want to do is make Brian feel like I can't handle all this. I don't know what's wrong with me right now. I feel *off*. It's as though that switch inside me never flipped at all, and I'm still the same Mina I was when I first came to the house.

When he's gone, I grab a glass of champagne and some tiny food off a passing tray and watch the room.

Nearly half an hour has passed, and I've lost sight of Windsor and worry he's gone to follow Brian. I put the empty glass down, intent on following him, when I'm stopped.

"You're with Brian Sloan, aren't you?" a man with an indiscernible accent says.

"Who's asking?" I continue to scan the ballroom, not sure if I'm looking for Windsor or Brian, but I can't go after Brian now. What if this guy follows?

"Dante Valentino," he says with a small insincere bow.

I stiffen and smile tightly at him. I wonder if he knows Brian agreed to kill him for Windsor. How would he?

I'm so tired of these games.

Dante moves in close to me and grips my arm too tightly. He leans in, his voice a low growl. "Time's up. I want Windsor gone tonight, or I'm going to become very unreasonable."

He allows his gaze to sweep over my body. Oh, this man is a dead man. If Brian doesn't kill him, I surely will. Unfortunately I don't have weapons on me. We've been in the ballroom this entire time, and the weapons are... not in the ballroom.

"I'm sorry, but I don't know what you're talking about. I'm only accompanying Mr. Sloan for the evening," I say, playing into the escort rumor and trying to sound as stupid and vapid as possible.

I relax when I feel Brian behind me, his hands sliding around my waist.

"Brian," Dante says, nodding. "Good to see you. I trust everything is in order."

I'm sure Brian nods, and probably gives Dante a glare for good measure, but I don't see him because I'm still looking at Dante. My breath comes in sharply, as Brian presses a kiss to the side of my throat, then he takes my hand to lead me away.

"You too have fun, tonight," Dante says with a weird creepy laugh.

"Let's kill him," I say under my breath.

Brian only chuckles, as he leads me through the crowd. I admire the view of his broad back in the tuxedo, and suddenly I'm thinking about getting it off of him.

He guides me down several hallways, and I allow myself to be pulled inside one of the rooms.

"Where are we?" I ask. The room is dark except for the small strips of moonlight coming in.

Brian pushes me against the wall, his mouth on mine, and my nerves slowly slide away as his hands move down my body.

## CHAPTER 9

# BRIAN

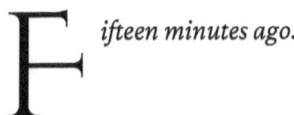

F ifteen minutes ago.

I HAVEN'T BEEN able to get Windsor alone all evening. I had thought it would be easy to lure him away, but his security detail tonight is even more intense than it was on the night of the cocktail party. And he's constantly got important people around him wanting to discuss important things. So he certainly has no time for the likes of me. It would look suspicious if he put these people off to talk to a complete stranger who doesn't seem particularly important in comparison to themselves.

I grab a gun and one of the knives my target allowed me to hide throughout the house. I was careful to stash weapons without marks or prints, that hadn't been used in any kill before, with no provenance or traceability. I get all my weapons on the dark web... mostly ghost guns, but some are standard with the serial numbers filed off. Every bullet was inserted with gloves on, so not even a fingerprint on a shell casing will be left behind. I have thought of everything, just in case there's some sort of double cross waiting for me.

I would never blindly trust that I could just leave weapons at his house. I made sure there was no security footage rolling—or hidden cameras—while I planted them, and I've checked again tonight to make sure the state of things remains the same. Everything is clear and clean and ready. The only problem is, I can't get the target alone. If I thought it would do any good, I'd try to get Mina to seduce him into my trap.

Dante is at this party. I don't know why he'd accept an invitation from his target when they seem locked in this tug-of-war of who can kill who first. Nothing about any of this smells right, but it's far too late to pull the plug. Plus I don't want to. I feel genuine glee at the prospect of killing Drake Windsor tonight. And Halloween is the only holiday I like. The one night of the year that celebrates death and puts a glittering orange bow on it, so of course I have to celebrate with blood.

I slip away from the party and make my way to the second floor study. I wasn't kidding about that fountain pen. It'll be my most extravagant trophy so far. Maybe I'll use it to write the condolence card for the flowers I send to his funeral. I slip on a pair of black gloves before trying the door. I don't expect it to be unlocked, but I try anyway.

It's not. I retrieve a lock picking kit from my pocket and get to work. A few minutes later I'm in. I open the drawer to find the Montblanc pen inside its case. The last time I killed for Windsor, he told me about the history of this pen. It is one of only 81 ever made after the death of Prince Rainier of Monaco. The body of the pen is 18k white gold and there are eight carats worth of inlaid diamonds and rubies. Incredibly this is far from the most expensive fountain pen in the world, but it still irritates me that anyone would own such a thing.

I take the case with the pen and slip it in my inside jacket pocket. I've just stepped out into the hallway when I find Drake

Windsor himself coming out of the bathroom... without his security detail. He slipped his own guard for the pleasure of a few short moments of freedom to piss in peace, and here we are.

He eyes me warily, sizing up what to him probably now looks like a hungry wolf seeing dinner. I think for a moment that he'll run. It would be the wisest choice, but I'd still catch him. I'm far younger and in far better shape.

"Sloan, you surprised me. Have you done it yet?"

"No, not yet. Just about to."

He takes a step back that I don't think he's even conscious he's taken. I reach out and grab him by the collar and shove him back into the bathroom, shutting and locking the door behind me.

"Brian, what... why? It's nine million dollars. Dante is only paying you two!"

"You know about the contract?"

"Of course I know. I have a mole inside Dante's organization. He isn't as smart as he thinks he is."

"Well, judging by your current predicament, neither are you."

I hold him by the throat against the wall. He claws at me, but he can't even escape my weaker hand.

"If you had a mole, why didn't you get *him* to kill Dante?"

He struggles to speak, and I ease the pressure on his throat enough so he can get the words out.

"B-because he's not... a killer like you. He would have gotten caught. He would have squealed. I needed a professional who could do it right. I thought you'd take the higher contract. That's all you care about. You have no honor."

My jaw clenches at this piece of shit even thinking to pass judgment on me, knowing what he is underneath his bespoke suits, ridiculous pens, and rare car collection.

"The offer is still on the table. You have no reason to be loyal to Dante. He's making a mockery of you. He offered the contract to someone else if he could get to me before you, it's why my security detail has been so tight for the last several weeks. And I know I can't make him an offer. This guy would kill me for free."

So would I. But I don't say this out loud.

"Who?" I growl, tightening my grip on his throat.

"Gregor McDonald."

Fuck. Fuck. Fuck.

If Gregor can't get to Windsor, he'll take the next best thing.

"That woman with you? She's not an escort is she?" Windsor says, mirroring my own thoughts.

His eyes widen when I pull out my knife. "You let me hide the weapon that was going to kill you inside your own house, you stupid motherfucker."

"I don't understand. I've done nothing to you! We've always been on friendly terms. Dante is making a joke of you and your reputation. He sent Gregor after me for fuck's sake. Just take the money and take out the true threat."

"I am taking out the threat. I saw the sick shit on your computer. The sad part though? If you hadn't left me alone in your study to find it, I would have taken your offer and taken out Dante instead. You could be breathing happy free air right now without a target over your head if you weren't so fucking cavalier about your own crimes."

"W-w-wait! I can't explain."

I have no interest in hearing Drake Windsor's pathetic explanations. I drive the knife into his gut, stabbing him over and over until his screams stop and he slumps forward.

I look around frantically. This wasn't part of any version of this plan. I haul the body into the tub and pull the curtain around it. I'm surprised this bathroom doesn't have a more modern glass-walled shower or a free standing tub with no curtain at all, but it's one of likely thirty bathrooms in this house. They can't all be architectural magazine porn. I scrub my hands and the knife in the sink, then sheath the blade and return it to its holster.

I let out a sigh of relief when I find bleach under the sink. I scrub the tiles and all the places where blood splattered. I open the window to air out the noxious bleach smell, then I take a look at my own clothes. All the blood hit the jacket, nothing on the shirt. I scrub at it to get out as much as I can, but it isn't noticeable against the black fabric.

I lock the bathroom door behind me, hoping no one else will stray this far from the party before I can get this all cleaned up.

# CHAPTER 10
# MINA

Brian pulls me against him in the darkened room, his mouth finding mine. I gasp, a tiny moan escaping me as I melt into his kiss. I'm about to ask about the target we still haven't taken out when the door clangs against the wall, and I jump, spinning as the light flicks on. A masked man in a tuxedo fills the doorway.

Brian's hand moves possessively up the back of my neck, gripping me. I expect him to move in front of me, to protect me from the intruder, but he doesn't.

Finally, after what feels like my entire lifetime up until this moment, the man in the doorway speaks. "Mina, what in the hell do you think you're doing with him?"

I try to spin around, but the man who now clearly isn't Brian, has a grip on the back of my neck so tight I can't move.

Brian removes his mask and puts it in the pocket of his jacket, then his eyes move away from me dismissively and on to the stranger. I feel suddenly like everything between us is gone in an instant—as though it was only ever a mirage.

"Brian?"

But he doesn't look at me. It's like I'm dead to him. My heartbeat picks up, thrumming faster and louder until my entire body is vibrating with the energetic pulses of life that could be taken from me at any time. I have never before been aware of just how close to death I live than in this moment. It's as though my heart knows it's almost over and is rushing to fit in as many beats as possible while it still can.

I've always known what Brian was—the monster he really is when he isn't with me—and sometimes when he is with me—but I've never had the weight of his nature truly aimed in my direction. I thought I knew his darkness, his coldness, but if I thought I went to bed with death at night, I was adorably naive about what that meant.

This is Brian. The *real* Brian. The one he shields me from. And I didn't realize until this moment just how much he still shielded me from what he is.

I feel like I'm meeting this man for the very first time—like my first night at the Pleasure House when he terrified me so much... except this is somehow so much worse because back then, he was intrigued by me. I may not have known it at the time but that's what it was. And now...? He's flipped that switch inside himself— the switch I never thought would be flipped on me. I was so stupid, dancing with the devil all this time—thinking somehow I was special, that his danger and darkness would never turn on me and that the death he wears like a shroud would never wrap its icy fingers around my throat.

Because I was special. I was so incredibly wrong.

"Brian, I didn't know, I thought it was you."

He chuckles humorlessly. "You thought it was me, Mina? You can't tell the difference in my kiss and a stranger's? Let's not kid ourselves here." There's an edge of barely controlled rage in his voice, and the combination of his ice and his fire aimed at me is almost more than I can take.

"Everyone's wearing a mask! The party was crowded. And..." I trail off, stopping myself in time because I don't know how Brian would react to what I was about to say.

"And what, Mina? What lies are about to fall out of your faith-less mouth?"

"He felt cold and empty... like you."

I see the slightest flicker of something behind Brian's eyes, but it's gone in the next second.

He turns his attention back to the man I can't see, the man I so stupidly thought was Brian. I get it. I understand why this seems so unbelievable, that I wouldn't know my own lover's touch, that I wouldn't be able to discern Brian's lips on my throat or on my mouth from a stranger's. But he *felt* like him. All I know right now is that I'm alone in a room with two killers.

"Well, this takes the fun out of everything," the stranger says.

"Gregor, how have you been?" Brian says. His tone is calm, casual. He knows this guy? Of course he does. They both carry the same energy, like they were inducted into the same secret society murder club together.

"I can't complain," Gregor says.

"The target is dead, and I already sent proof. The money has been wired to my account. I was going to take Mina on a nice trop-ical holiday, but... tonight has reminded me... I work better alone."

Gregor's grip tightens on the back of my neck. "I'll kill her." It's painfully clear that he had a script and can't keep up with the change that makes the script irrelevant now. I realize suddenly that the history between these two isn't pleasant. This guy lured me away with the plan to what? Fuck what belongs to Brian? Kill me? Kill me while Brian watched? Did Dante know it wasn't Brian leading me away from the party?

Brian rolls his eyes. "Did you miss the last couple of minutes? I don't give a flying fuck. Fuck her, torture her, kill her. What the fuck do I care? She's not mine anymore. She's nothing to me. I would sell her to you, to try to recoup some of my losses—and frankly this contract is only a third of what I paid for her—but given the bad blood between you and I, I think it's a pretty even trade. I'll take the monetary loss and we can let bygones be bygones."

"Brian... I swear I didn't know... please. Master," my voice cracks on that last word.

I see the muscle in his jaw tighten, but he ignores me.

"Master?" Gregor says. "What kind of kinky games do you two have going on behind the scenes?"

"It's not a game," Brian says. "I bought this worthless little whore, if you can believe it. She's my *actual* real property. I paid five million for her."

Gregor laughs. "If you paid that much, then she must be worth it." The thumb of the hand gripping me so tightly begins to caress the side of my throat. "I bet you're a smooth, slick ride, aren't you, honey? Maybe I'll fuck you before I kill you. Would you like that? I'll make you moan my name while I sink my cock so deep inside you, you'll forget all about Sloan, here. And who knows... maybe if you're a good enough lay, I'll keep you alive for a while."

I look to Brian, hoping this is all just some kind of ruse to rescue me, but he is a wall of ice, completely shut off to me—emotionless. Surely these words from his rival would soften him, or give me even the tiniest hint that this is all some plan he has.

"Master... please. I swear I didn't know. I'm yours, you know I'm yours. I love you."

I'm not sure I've ever said these words out loud to him, at least not explicitly. I've held them close inside. They have always felt like such foolish words to say to a man like Brian. I know he cares for me... or... I thought he did, but I'm not sure love is a thing he's capable of—even for me. And especially now, in light of this new unfolding situation.

I'm not sure he can work past the anger and betrayal he feels to get to a rational thought long enough to remember what we are to each other.

Finally he turns back to me and laughs. "It's a convenient time to address me properly, isn't it? A very convenient time to express your undying love, when you know you're about to die. You haven't really been mine for a long time, and we both know it, Mina." He practically spits those last words out at me.

I know what he means. His ownership of me has been little more than a performance at the house since I rescued him from Matsumoto's son at Easter. That feels like a lifetime ago.

The dynamic between us shifted irrevocably. I thought he was okay with it. I thought he was on board and that power flowing back and forth between us in a more balanced way was what he wanted.

Maybe not.

"So, it wouldn't bother you then if I fucked her right in front of you before I killed her?" Gregor says.

This is not going at all according to his plan. He thought Brian would try to bargain for my life. Gregor no doubt had some big revenge plot playing through his head, but Brian's cold indifference wasn't at all what he expected or hoped.

I'm still trying to hold onto the frail hope that this IS some plan to rescue me from a dangerous situation, but if Gregor is buying it, and he's like Brian, then maybe it's the truth.

They all turn on me in the end. They all hurt me. I should have known Brian would be no different, but he *seemed* so different. I thought we had something real, but Brian is a sociopath. I've forgotten that fact a thousand times in his arms. He has no soul, no conscience. Everything is a mask, a game to him. He is an actor on the stage of life, perfectly playing his part. But the man who plays the character I've grown to love... that's the man I'm faced with right now, and he is *nothing* like the character he plays.

"Not at all," Brian says. "In fact, we should fuck and kill her together. Put the past in the past."

My ears are ringing as every piece of his carefully crafted mask slips away and all I'm left with is the monster underneath.

Brian stalks me, his fierce black gaze locked on mine, as though he could consume me and burn me to ashes with only a look.

"Are you ready to take us both like a good little whore? Be good, and maybe he'll keep you. I've certainly got no use for you anymore. You cramp my style."

Tears stream down my face, and I shudder as Gregor's other

hand begins to drift down my back as the zipper slides down inch by creeping inch.

"Master…" I can't beg him again because I know it won't matter. I can't break past this wall he's erected between us.

Gregor finally lets go of the back of my neck, as he begins to move his hands slowly over me.

I look to Brian, hoping to see the tiniest flicker of any emotion that exists in the whole gradient of human feelings. But he's empty. I've lost him. I can't believe I've lost this one person I thought I'd have forever.

"Kiss me like it's your last time, Mina, because it is." Brian grips the back of my neck and pulls me into him. When our lips touch I feel all the coldness he's held back from me, but I also feel intensity, passion, fire, anger. There are so many contradicting things inside this kiss, I can't name them all, and I don't understand how they all exist together.

The tears flow harder down my cheeks as his… friend? enemy? begins to kiss a trail down my back, and I shudder against the mouth I can't believe I thought was Brian's. This one miscalculation will cost me everything.

Then, a moment later, Gregor isn't touching me anymore. I hear his body slump to the floor. I startle and turn to find an empty syringe in Brian's hand. It clatters to the ground and he pulls me into him, just holding me, and I can feel his heart pounding against me. My heart beats just as hard, and it's as though our two hearts are tiny panicked birds, flapping against the walls of our cages trying desperately to get to each other.

"I really thought it was you. I'm sorry, I know it was stupid. I…"

He pulls back from me and all the coldness has dropped away.

"I know, baby. But I once killed the woman he loved. He would have snapped your neck before I reached you. I'm sorry I had to go so cold. It was the only way he'd believe me. Anything less than a perfect show would have gotten you killed."

I can't stop crying.

I look up and our eyes meet. "It was a really convincing show," I say.

Brian brushes a strand of hair out of my eyes and smirks. "What's Halloween without a little scare?"

I feel his hard length pressed against me, and I wonder what part of this entire situation has him so worked up.

He wipes the tears off my face with the pads of his thumbs while he holds me like I'm the oxygen that makes his life possible. And I let out a long slow, steadying breath.

"What about him?" I ask, nodding at Gregor.

# CHAPTER 11
# BRIAN

I leave Mina alone in the room to gather myself, under the guise of getting something to transport Gregor. I've got about an hour before the drug wears off, and I want to be fully set up before that happens.

Everything inside me is racing around, panicked, angry, unsettled, buzzing with worries and lists inside my head, but outwardly I'm the glassy surface of a lake, completely unperturbed.

A thousand emotions fight for dominance. Nothing has gone according to my plan tonight. Why make such elaborate plans if they crumple to dust at the first interaction with the real world? I don't regret taking out the target when and how I did—you don't return a gift like that to the universe unopened—but it feels like a million tiny loose threads that I can't tie back together, and everything inside my brain is a chaotic storm.

Then there's the lingering fear of what could have happened to Mina if I hadn't gotten there in time, if I hadn't been convincing enough to get close and get Gregor distracted enough to sink that needle into his throat. I can't let my mind go there. I don't know what would happen if I ever lost her.

I love having a partner to do this with. I never thought I would, but I do. But maybe I'm being selfish putting her into all this risk and danger. For what? To fulfill some latent Bonnie and Clyde fantasy? We all know how that story turned out.

And then... there's the cold anger, a gnarled and twisted thing resting in the pit of my stomach. However irrational, that anger is at Mina for allowing herself to be lured away by a rival. For kissing him. For not knowing it was me. Rationally I get it. Adrenaline is high. I get how he could feel a lot like me. We have a similar build, same hair color, same eye color. Logically I know, but there is a part of me so angry at her, and that anger terrifies me because though I may do dark and twisted things, my rage has always felt very controlled to me—even if it's felt chaotic to others.

My rage doesn't feel controlled right now. Now that the danger has passed I'm not sure I trust myself to be in the same room with her. I take a long deep breath. This is not what I need to be focused on right now. I need to finish this and get us safely off the radar before bodies are discovered.

I can still salvage part of the plan, it'll just be used on a different person. I put my mask back on and go up to the second floor bathroom. I'd planned not to return here, and this feels far too dangerous. There's a risk of being interrupted, and returning to the scene of a crime is never a good thing, but I have a new plan forming.

The bathroom door is still locked and undisturbed from the last time I was here. I take one more quick look before picking the lock.

Once safely inside, I secure the door again. The bleach smell is mostly gone. I studied the entire layout of this house for countless hours during early planning, and I'm ninety percent sure I know what's outside under this window. I lean out into the crisp fall night air and am rewarded with the sight of giant holly bushes. Perfect. And it's on the back side of the house which no one is watching at the moment. Why would they? All the real ways into the house are closer to the front, and the Windsor Estate's entire security detail is focused on the logistics of the party as Windsor promised they would be.

I pull back the shower curtain and let out a relieved breath when I see the body still right where I left it. Did I expect it to get up and move? With the way this night is going? Nothing would surprise me.

I remove his glasses and put them in my pocket, then I drag Windsor out of the bathtub and push him out the window, watching to make sure the body is completely covered by the shrubbery and no stray pieces of his clothes or any limbs are hanging out.

I nod, satisfied that everything is well concealed. I get the bleach and clean out the tub where he finished bleeding out. I leave the window cracked to air out the room again. With any luck no one will even step inside this bathroom until tomorrow. I make sure there's no remaining evidence in the bathroom, then I slip downstairs to a small room near the kitchen and pull mine and Mina's change of clothes from their hiding spot. I change into the staff uniform and go to the kitchen to get the rolling cart.

When I return to Mina, I toss the other bag of clothes to her. "Change," I say. My tone is abrupt, and I find I can't look at her. Now that the immediate danger is gone, I just... can't.

She hurriedly changes out of the formal evening gown and into the clothes she normally wears when we go on these jobs together. The dress is a slinky material and seems to convert to a liquid when she puts it in the bag.

My jaw clenches as I imagine Gregor peeling that dress off her and fucking her. Had that been his intention? To defile her in the barely-lit room before I discovered them? He *was* kissing her after all. And she was letting him do it. I take another measured breath. She didn't know it wasn't me. But it doesn't matter how much I repeat this truth to myself. Surely some part of her had to know. Some dark place within her that she can't acknowledge.

Am I not monster enough for her now? Before the changes in her, I never would have thought that she needed a monster in her life. Unlike the pieces of shit who had her before me, I've never believed she somehow wants a man who hurts her. Out of all the men in the world I was the least likely to be safe for her. And yet... here we are. But am I still safe? Am I enough for her?

I don't know if I need to be more man or more monster to keep her, and that thought enrages me. She cost me millions to possess, but what if at the end of it all, I can't keep her heart? I hate that I'm thinking these things, feeling these things. What the fuck is wrong with me that I should care about any of this?

I want to punish her for kissing him. For making me feel all these things I can't process. For making me doubt myself. For twisting me up into this sad hybrid creature... not quite a man, but not quite a monster—a least not with her anymore.

"Grab his feet," I say when she's fully changed. Mina grabs Gregor's feet and I grip under his shoulders, then we neatly transport my new prey onto the bottom of the rolling cart. I cover it again with the long white tablecloth and roll him out to the location we set up for the original target.

An hour has passed when my captive starts to wake and slowly rise up out of his groggy haze. I've got him chained up in the conservatory, several acres away from the main property. With everyone at the party, and the dark blanket of night wrapping around the gardens, it's unlikely anyone will be out here again until sunrise... unless...

Just outside the conservatory, the Windsor Estate has a large pumpkin patch. It's just the kind of place a couple of lovers might slip off to in order to get away from the party. But at least for now, it seems no one has been tempted by the call of a pumpkin patch on Halloween. I guess nobody believes in The Great Pumpkin anymore.

Windsor's body is slumped in the corner of the conservatory. I went back for him once I got Gregor secured. I want all my bodies in one place for tonight.

Mina helped, but we still haven't really spoken—not since my initial relief at her safety. I think she senses something is very off about me, and I pray silently to any dark god who might hear my prayers that what I'm about to do will sate the beast inside demanding she be punished—that I can get all my rage out on Gregor and spare Mina my simmering wrath.

I get tired of waiting for him to fully wake up and slap him across the face. After another few seconds, his vision finally clears and he stares at me, his eyes narrowing.

"I knew it! I fucking *knew* you were bluffing!"

"Yeah," I agree. "It was Old Man Whittaker the whole time, Scooby. If you *knew*, you wouldn't be in these chains right now."

His gaze drops to a side table and his eyes widen when he notices the hockey mask and chainsaw. What? It's Halloween. I'm going to paint the room with this piece of shit's intestines, and I'm far enough away from the delicate ears of witnesses that I get to use a chainsaw to do it. I am giddy with delight.

"Brian…" he says, his tone warning. As though he's in any position to warn me about anything.

"You shouldn't have tried to steal my contract out from under me. And you *really* shouldn't have touched what's mine. The first thing I might have been able to let go but not the second. In deference to you being a work colleague, I'll make it quick."

I put on a pair of black gloves then pick up the hockey mask and secure it in place, a thrilling rush of adrenaline surging through me. Nothing else exists right now except for me… and my prey. The only thing that matters in this moment is the kill and finding out just how much blood I can squeeze out of this motherfucker. It's sort of a macabre version of: Guess how many jelly beans are in the jar.

"Brian! Wait! If you care about her so much, you must know why I did it. You killed Vanessa!"

"She was in the wrong place at the wrong time."

"I loved her! You know how hard it is for men like you and I to feel anything at all. And you took her from me."

"Awww, such a sad story. I don't care," I say flatly. And I don't. If he'd loved her so much he never would have let her fall into my path. It was simple enough to keep his kitty indoors. I ignore the judge in my head that convicts me for this same crime. I could have left Mina at home, out of harms way, and we wouldn't even be here right now.

I shake my head, clearing it of all these encroaching thoughts seeking to pull me from my moment of bliss, and start up the chainsaw. Gregor tries to say more. He tries to plead more for his life, to reason with me.

"What's that?" I shout over the noise. "Can't hear you."

## CHAPTER 12
# MINA

S omething isn't right about Brian. And I'm not too proud to admit that I'm a little scared right now. Maybe it's spillover from his very convincing performance, but I feel like there's more to it than that. After that moment where he held me and expressed probably as much emotion as Brian is capable of, he shut down again, and the wall was back firmly in place. He was all business, barking out orders.

I helped him with all the parts I could do and tried not to let it disturb me. After all, the plan once again has gone south, and we're left having to form a new plan mid-game.

By the time he wakes Gregor, I don't think he even realizes I'm here. I melt into the shadows, quietly watching the exchange. I feel a jolt of terror as he puts the hockey mask on and picks up the chainsaw. His eyes meet mine through the mask for the briefest moment, and I go back in time to my childhood and all the scary movies that looked very much like this.

It's easy to forget sometimes what Brian is. It's a combination of the way he treats me and how we're always a team—on the same side. But he's the horror movie monster calmly and relentlessly stalking his prey. There's no doubt about that right now.

Ever since that switch flipped in me, and I became so much

more like Brian than I want to admit, none of this has bothered me. The blood. The gore. The sadism. Unless it's one of the girls at the house, it doesn't affect me, and more often than not, I want to join in on the fun.

But tonight, everything feels different. It's as though this night where the veil is thin has allowed a piece of the old me to rise from the dead, dragging and pulling itself out of the grave to walk for this one final night. Parts of that scared girl are working to fight their way to the surface, and now is a really bad time for that. I feel like I'm hovering just above myself watching this scene play out because it's too hard to stand in this room with such a dark swirling energy of death and destruction as Brian.

I flinch when the chainsaw starts up.

The screams don't last long. It's hard to stretch that out with Brian's weapon of choice. He's only lopped off the first arm when Gregor goes into shock, and then he's quickly gone as Brian hacks the body into more pieces than it probably needs to be in.

Windsor's body is too close to where Brian is working and is now covered with Gregor's blood.

"That's enough!" I shout. I don't know what possesses me to interrupt him, but he's out of control. This isn't Brian. This isn't how he normally is. Gregor is in far more pieces than he needs to be in, and I'm sure if I don't break through to him and stop him, he'll just keep going until the chainsaw doesn't have a piece of flesh and bone big enough to cut through. I am keenly aware of how much mess this is to clean up, and how much evidence is filling up this small space with each passing second.

He turns slowly back toward me, the mask still in place, the chainsaw still running. He's covered in so much blood, and then he starts to walk toward me with purpose. And I panic.

I turn, and run. I hear the chainsaw revving behind me as he chases me. Is he even still in there at all? Is he going to hack me up, too? Ordinarily such a thought would never enter my mind, but he's gone somewhere inside himself. Is he even in control at all? Who or what is in the driver's seat right now? Is he in some kind of trance he can't break free from? What does that mean for me?

This is the first night in longer than I can remember that I have actually been scared of Brian. Not just scared—bone chillingly terrified of him. Am I really about to be hacked up in the middle of a pumpkin patch on Halloween?

What a tragic end to our story.

The pumpkin patch goes on forever, and I'm weaving in and out of the largest pumpkins I've ever seen. The sound of the saw gets closer and closer until it goes silent. I hear the now quiet weapon land on the ground a moment before Brian is on me. We fall together in the fat leaves between the pumpkins.

I look up at him. He's covered in blood, still wearing the hockey mask. His gloved hand strays to my throat, and I feel the wetness of his victim's blood against my skin. I can barely breathe, and it's not because he's squeezing, he isn't. It's that I'm not sure if I remember how to breathe. He pulls his hand back and tilts his head to the side like a curious puppy.

Did he just intentionally leave a bloody handprint on me? Did he just mark me with his prey's blood? What in the fuck is going on right now?

"Brian?" I say, my voice wavering, hoping he'll snap out of whatever the hell this is.

But he doesn't. He just flips me over onto my hands and knees and pulls down my pants and panties. A moment later, his hand cracks hard against my ass, and then I hear the zipper of his own pants. I grab at the ground to steady myself in this surreal moment. He doesn't trust himself to fuck me, and yet... here he is. He really has lost himself.

I gasp when he grips my hips and thrusts into me. And then I start to cry, but it's relief—not fear or pain. Because when his body is seated deep inside of mine, everything feels right in the world again. I feel that connection between us reforming, the threads weaving back together. He rips my corset off, and his gloved hand presses against my back as he drives into me harder. The warmth of his body steadies me and helps me breathe again.

And then he's pulling me back against him, his hands coming around me to cup and stroke my breasts. I must be covered in Gregor's blood by now. A needy moan leaves me. He only fucks me harder in response.

I feel his mouth on my throat, kissing and sucking and biting at the tender flesh, like some wild animal with a meaty bone. Then his mouth is at my ear and he says the first words he's said to me since this sequence of terror began.

"This is what my mouth on you feels like, Mina. Remember it for next time."

My only reply is a whimper as he continues to drive into me. We are rutting like two animals out under the stars and full moon, both of our pleasure climbing higher and higher until it explodes. If his groan is any indication, he comes right after me. And then we collapse together.

I pant, trying to catch my breath, then I pull myself up and lean against one of the pumpkins. Brian moves closer to me, his arms wrapped around me, his head pressed against the center of my chest, no doubt listening to my raging heart as it gallops along like a wild horse. I'm not sure when he took the mask off, but it's on the ground near the chainsaw.

We stay together like this for a long time, until finally, I break the silence.

"Brian?"

"Yeah?" he says quietly.

The anger I thought he had toward me left him in the frantic primal nature of our coupling.

"How are we going to clean all this up?"

"We aren't. Come with me." He stands and helps me up, then he picks up my clothes and hands them to me.

I dress quietly as he retrieves the mask and chainsaw. I watch as he inspects the leaves we were in and tears off a few covered in blood. He buries those in the dirt and rearranges everything so it doesn't look like anyone was ever here.

I follow him back to the conservatory. He takes a cloth and wipes down some things. I watch as he puts the hockey mask on Windsor's face and gets the man's fingerprints on the chainsaw before dropping it near the pieces of Gregor.

"Where's the knife you stabbed Windsor with? This will never work," I say.

He chuckles. "It's in its holster. I'm just sowing confusion, Killer."

"Why not just clean up and get rid of the bodies? Why leave a scene to be discovered at all?"

Brian looks up sharply at me. "Because while the police may not know who Gregor is, the underworld circles I run in, do. They need to know there are consequences to trying to pull a contract out from under me. I told Dante it would get done. Besides, Windsor has underage porn all over his computer. The police will at least find that, and then it won't seem so strange that he'd do something so monstrous as this even if nothing about it looks quite right. Are we done with the Q&A portion of the evening?"

I nod while Brian takes care of the last remaining details to set the scene and wipes down a few more things we may have touched.

He leads me around to the side of the building outside and turns on a water hose.

"Strip," he says.

"You can't be serious."

"I am. We need to get out of these clothes and clean up if we're going to leave without drawing suspicion."

There is a crisp chill in the air, but I know he's right. I strip and he hoses me down, careful not to get my hair wet. I'm surprised when he tosses me a towel.

"Where did you get this?"

"One of the hall bathrooms when I was getting the rolling cart."

"What about the cart?"

"I'll handle it."

By the time I'm dry, Brian has removed his own clothes. "Now do me."

I spray him clean. The hockey mask protected his face from blood, so it's just his body we have to worry about. I try not to ogle and wonder if he ogled me when our positions were reversed. He's in mission mode, so probably not, but I do appreciate the view of water sliding down all those perfectly formed muscles even if they are the muscles of an unrepentant killer.

I toss him my towel to dry off. He changes back into the staff uniform and takes the rolling cart back to the house. I put my masquerade mask and evening gown back on and carry our bags. One of the bags has Brian's tux and mask, the other contains the clothes from tonight we'll have to incinerate.

By the time he's returned the cart and changed clothes, the party is winding down. We blend into the throng of people leaving, and get into Brian's nondescript black sedan parked in a row of other nondescript black sedans.

No one seems to have yet missed their host. By the time they realize he's gone, we'll be back at the house burning the last of the evidence.

# CHAPTER 13
# MINA

The drive is long and quiet. Brian is tense, and I'm tense because he's tense. Finally it's too much for me.

"Are you okay?" I ask.

His grip tightens on the steering wheel, his knuckles going white. "No, I am not fucking okay."

He sounds broken, and I don't know what to do with this version of Brian. Nor do I understand it. It can't be killing those guys. Even with the chainsaw, in a lot of ways it was standard operating procedure for Brian—even if it got a little weird.

My hand strays to rest on his thigh. One of his hands leaves the steering wheel and covers mine.

"Now do you understand why I don't trust myself to fuck you?" he asks, his tone grave.

"Not really, no."

"Mina, for fuck's sake, you were crying, and I just kept fucking you. Those weren't tears of pleasure. I didn't even care. I heard it, and I didn't care, I just wanted to be inside you and mark you as mine. This compulsive need to mark you is going to get you killed. I was punishing you because I was so angry that you'd let Gregor touch you, that you'd been fooled by him. Even though I know it's

68

irrational, and you didn't do anything wrong. I don't trust myself and how possessive I am of you. I don't trust your safety with me."

"They were tears of relief," I say. "I wasn't upset you were fucking me."

He pulls his hand away from mine and puts it back on the steering wheel. It seems to take his every ounce of self-control to do this.

"Oh, that's so much better, Mina. You were relieved I wasn't about to chainsaw massacre you, so rough fucking was just fine by comparison."

I remain quiet because there's nothing I can say to deny his accusation. I *had* been afraid he was going to kill me with that chainsaw.

"You weren't yourself. You were out of control."

"Yeah. I know. I was there. Once again, this is why I don't trust myself to fuck you. This is why the only way we can do it is if you chain me up like the rabid dog I am. You have no idea the fucked-up thoughts that were spinning through my mind when I was chasing you. Nothing will ever make tonight okay, so don't fucking try to sugarcoat it. Don't forgive me or act like it's no big deal because it's a very big fucking deal. You not being traumatized by it, doesn't change the wrongness of my end of it."

"So, what? Are you going to break up with me?" I ask. I'm being a smart ass, but I don't like how it feels like he's pulling away, like he wants to shelve our entire relationship because he doesn't trust himself. What about what I want?

"Never," he growls.

"Well okay then."

Another couple of miles of dark interstate passes by the windows before I speak again.

"I liked it."

"Mina, don't say that."

"I did. I liked you all wild and primal and dark. I didn't think you would ever hurt me. I just knew something strange had happened to you. I wasn't sure YOU were in control, but as long as you are in control of you, I trust you. I trust us."

"You shouldn't. I'm a wild animal. I should be locked away in a cage."

I sigh and stare out the window. We don't speak again for the rest of the ride back to the house. It's late when we get back. A couple of Jack-o-Lanterns glow on the front porch. I hear shrieks and screams outside, but they aren't horror movie screams. They're the sounds of people playing out by the pool.

Brian and I walk around to the side of the house. There's a raging bonfire in the back, a nighttime picnic set up with burgers and hot dogs, and lots of splashing in the heated pool under halloween orange lights that have been strung all around it.

Brian leans in and whispers in my ear, "Wouldn't you have rather been at this party than the one you ended up at with me?"

"No," I say, and go back to the front door. I hold the door open for Brian so he can carry our bags in.

We go down to the incinerator first and burn the bag with the bloody clothes. Then we stand in our shared dungeon room and just stare at each other. It's as though we're suddenly strangers, and I hate it. I hate this distance he's put between us. He may mean to protect me, but it only hurts me.

"Brian..." I start to move closer to him. I want to close this distance between us before it becomes a sinkhole that swallows us both.

He shakes his head and holds up a hand as though warding me away. "Mina, I need you to do something for me."

"Anything."

"I need you to punish me. For tonight."

"I told you, I'm not upset about tonight."

"Yeah? Well I am. And I'm not ever going to get the fuck over it until I feel like I've paid for what I did to you."

"You didn't do anything to me!"

The muscle in Brian's jaw clenches. "You know that's not true. So will you do it?"

He holds my gaze, and there is so much pleading in his eyes. I've thought about this before. Not punishing him quite like this, and not domming him in the standard way, but giving him release from some of his demons. I know the power of that dungeon when used appropriately and the catharsis that can come when given the space to cry without someone asking 'What's wrong?'

I want to give that to Brian, because although I don't believe he deserves to be punished, I know he needs this for his own reasons.

"Will things go back to normal between us if I do?"

His dark gaze holds mine for a long time until finally he nods.

"Okay."

He lets out a breath. "Okay."

He walks past me out of our room.

"What? Right now?"

"Yes, right now, Mina. I need this right fucking now."

I follow him into Cell A, and he's already stripping down. When he's fully bare, he walks with purpose to the St. Andrew's Cross. He looks over his shoulder at me, a question in his gaze.

I let out a long breath. I can't believe we're here, that he isn't just letting me punish him, but actively asking for it. I don't know how to feel about any of this. I just need for things to go back the way they were between us before tonight.

I cross the room and secure his arms and legs. I trail my fingertips over the scars of his back—scars stretched and faded by time, given to him in his childhood. I press a kiss over one of the cigarette burn marks.

"What do you want me to use?" I ask quietly.

"Lady's choice."

I go to the large box of toys and implements and scan the various crops, whips and floggers hanging on hooks on the wall.

"Mina?"

"Yeah?"

"Do you remember how you were that day with the less impressive Matsumoto?"

I snort at this description. "Yes."

"I need you to be her."

"Okay."

I don't know what I'm going to use, but I feel so exposed with Brian watching me, so I take a black length of cloth from the box. I blindfold him and run my fingertip along his jawline.

"Let's let it be a surprise," I whisper.

I'm also offering him space and privacy for this. It's not lost on me the enormous amount of trust he's placing in me right now, to allow himself to be this vulnerable, to so utterly and completely reverse our roles—even if for only a moment.

Things have been different with us for a long time. I don't think either of us truly sees me as his slave anymore. It's an act we put on for the house—something which preserves Brian's reputation. It's a role I'm more than willing to play with the man who saved me in every way a person could be saved.

In private we're partners in crime, and in the bedroom the power flows back and forth between us with ease. But this is something else entirely. It's not the playful way we've been together, and I feel a duty to Brian to take this seriously. He's seeking penance, absolution, for a supposed crime I've already forgiven him for, but I'm worried he won't be able to forgive himself.

I run my fingertips over the supple leather of one of the whips. I select one and cross back over to Brian. I just stand there and stare at his back, hypnotized by the criss-crossing scars.

A long time passes.

"Mina?"

"I can't do this."

I expect him to get angry, but he just seems defeated as though the last hope of salvation has just passed him by. He's still blindfolded, and I take this moment to caress his jawline and kiss him. He opens to me and groans against my mouth. I know there are words bubbling to the surface, things he wants to say, but I keep him busy with my tongue's steady invasion.

Then I release him from the Saint Andrew's Cross and guide him back to our room.

I turn back to see him about to remove the blindfold.

"No," I say, my voice clipped and sharp.

I wait to see if he'll do as I ask. His free hand drops back to his side and he follows me where I guide him.

"Sit," I say, when he's in front of the bed, and he does.

I put the vinyl record on the turn table. The sound crackles gently just before Chopin's Nocturne number 2 begins to play.

I go to Brian's dresser and pull out clothes. I help him get dressed in a T-shirt and sweatpants and then socks and running shoes.

"Mina... running won't help this."

"Brian? Do I need to gag you?"

He hesitates a moment, but then shakes his head. He tenses when I sit on the bed beside him.

"I like the games we play," I begin. "I like that they flow in both directions now, but there is something light and playful about it. What you're asking me to do... I understand the logic behind it, and I thought I could do it for you, but I'm not willing to be your stepmother."

"That's not..."

"Yes it is."

Brian has been closed off for years, buried under the sociopathy that still protects that small boy inside him. But I'm not going to make him feel again with pain. I'm not going to be the next person who hurts him, no matter the justification.

I take his hand in mine. "I don't want our relationship to be based on hurting each other. There's no justification for this, and I'm not going to re-traumatize you based on some psychobabble armchair amateur shrink theories about healing through pain. I know you've done a lot of bad things, and I don't expect that to change. We both are what we both are at this point, but what we have together is different. It's special. And I'm not going to break that tonight over some misguided notion of you paying for a crime I haven't convicted you of."

"I carved the word *Mine* into your back, Mina. All we understand is pain."

"I know, but it was more about the marking than the pain. Did you do it because you like hurting me?"

I study his face, watching as he seems to be thinking it through to give me the real answer.

"No," he finally says.

"No. So let's go run."

"Running won't fix this," he says again.

I remove the blindfold and stare into his eyes. He doesn't try to look away. I don't think he realizes that I'm the only person he can do this with. Sure, he'll stare people down until they avert their gaze, but it's intimidation, not trust, not vulnerability.

I cross to my dresser and pull out my own gym clothes. He watches me as I change. I turn off the record, which has long since moved onto another Chopin piece. I extend my hand to him, he takes it, and we quietly go upstairs to the gym.

The party is still going on out at the pool. No one even knows we've returned to the house. We run together on the treadmill, and then I take him to the kitchen and make him some scrambled eggs just like he did for me the first time he shared this ritual with me—and many times after. Then we shower together, and by the time we're lying in bed, he seems more calm.

He moves up closer to me, his head leaned on my shoulder.

"We're going to be okay," I say.

"How do you know that?"

"I just do. I love you, Brian." I hate that the first time I said these words to him was when I thought he was about to let me die. But I'd needed him to know.

He's silent. I wish I could read the thoughts and fears inside his head. I know he can't say the words back, but a part of me believes he feels them even if he's never able to say them out loud. He reaches out and grips my hand in his, his thumb stroking slow circles over my skin.

And for now, that's enough.

# BEHIND THE SCENES
# WITH KITTY

Hello my little Candy Corns,

So here we are at the midpoint of the story arc for Brian and Mina's Holiday Hits. If you somehow stumbled upon this and are reading out of order, boy are you confused. If you want to know what you don't know, I suggest going back and reading Broken Dolls (book 2 in the Pleasure House World) and then starting this series from The Easter Hunt.

I had a little trouble deciding how to write this one and what exactly it would be about. I had another duet I wanted to write but I was stuck on that one, too, and I realized my brain was in this place where I was trying to commit to and write both of these stories at the same time (in totally different story worlds.)

While I've worked on more than one project before, this was different because these stories come out around the holidays, so there was pressure and a deadline attached. And while technically I can release them any time of the year, since it's unlikely once they're all out that people are going to just "wait for each holiday" considering that you need to read these novellas in order... still, it became important to me to release this "on time" in time for Halloween.

So I committed to this, still not knowing what the hell I was going to write. Though I DO have pretty much the whole plot for the fifth and final novella and a lot for the fourth (the next one: Yuletide Slay Ride). I guess necessity really is the mother of invention though, because once I committed to it and decided I was prioritizing finishing these novellas before I did anything else, the blurb started to form in my head, and from that... a story.

(I needed a blurb to order the print version!)

I had already written a snippet about the "tiny food" exchange, but had no other context. Since I already had the title, I knew this story would occur at Halloween at a Masquerade Ball. My mother named this book. She doesn't read my books because they are too dark and sexy for her, but she did come up with the name The Massacre Ball, which I love!

When I actually sat down to start writing this, The very first scene I wrote was the part where Brian shows up when Mina has been lured away and catches her with his rival. I wrote from that point to the end, then circled back to the beginning.

There is a LOT I love about this story. I love how back in Broken Dolls we learned that Brian sees a lot of his own suffering in Mina and because they have such similar physical scars, she becomes someone special under his protection. But now, he sees in Aidan a much closer version of his younger self, someone who shares very similar emotional scars, and he keeps feeling pulled back to this kid. He wants to protect Aidan from his own outcome.

With Mina the damage was already done, but if he could somehow help heal her, he thought he could undo his own trauma. And now he's stuck having only limited ability to stop the fate of this small boy that so closely mirrors his own. Aidan is like a true do-over, but with the same tragic consequences already written in his stars.

A strange family of killers is sort of coalescing around Brian as things go on, and it's both strangely sweet, and also so fucked up.

In the epilogue of Blowing Things Up, we know there is much more ahead when Aidan grows up, and there is the mention that

Brian has been in the shadows watching over him—like a hidden father figure. And in The Massacre Ball we get the first glimpse of this. Brian's stepmother's name also gets revealed for the first time, Linda.

I'm not sure if Brian was going to go through with it and kill the aunt, until she made the fatal mistake of burning him with a cigarette.

And like childhood Brian, Aidan has a dog—at least once he's gone to stay with his aunt. So I love this subplot that's developing in Brian's character arc that's allowing him to process certain emotions he was walled off from before. But my FAVORITE part of this one is the chainsaw massacre part... and when he chases Mina through the pumpkin patch.

And I know it is so beyond fucked up, but I love the moment where he leaves that bloody hand print on her throat and then cocks his head to the side like a confused cocker spaniel while still wearing that hockey mask. It's all pretty intense! Like what the FUCK is going on inside his head right now!

There is so much going on here... and if you're disappointed that scene was in Mina's head, it needed to be for a lot of different reasons. Don't worry, we are NOT done with this issue and you'll get Brian's POV about it all inside Yuletide Slay Ride.

The reason I love this part so much is how it ties back into the beginning, or technically I tied the beginning into it since I wrote the beginning after this scene was solidified (the benefits of writing books out of chronological order!)... wow this turned into a run on sentence... anyway... The reason I love this part so much is how it ties back to where Brian talks about how he doesn't like emotions going into a kill because when emotions are involved, that's when you fuck up.

This becomes a self-fulfilling prophecy when he kills his rival on Halloween night. His emotions are so out of control that something comes over him (that's all I'll say here about that, since I'll expand on it in the next one) and he chases Mina.

This—the hockey mask and chainsaw... the psycho killer

randomly killing without rhyme or reason—is the image he has of himself in his head and the monster he is and how ultimately dangerous he believes he is to her. Of course, he doesn't chainsaw massacre her, but the thoughts going through his mind in that scene are pretty dark. This also becomes the self-fulfilling prophecy of why he doesn't trust himself to fuck her unless she ties him up first, and how much he's tied this act into anger and punishing and how he's punishing her for things he knows aren't truly her fault.

This moment only reinforces all his fears and feelings about himself. So The Massacre Ball being the midpoint novella is Brian's black moment. I also think Brian can't tell Mina he loves her because if he says these words it all becomes real, and now he's got something he can lose—something others can use against him. Of course, it's already too late for that, but not saying these words is almost like some protective magic over her. Or over him. It's hard to tell which.

I knew early on that I wanted her to mistake Gregor for Brian and have things play out as they did, but I wasn't sure how exactly to do it so readers wouldn't see it coming. And I'm not sure if I succeeded, but I laid out a pattern of Brian coming up behind her and kissing her on the side of the neck so that when Gregor does it later, the reader would be less likely to question it. And Dante seems to add to the believability by confirming it's Brian.

So *did* Dante know it was Gregor? You'll find out in Yuletide Slay Ride!

Anyway, this is about all I have to say about this one!

There's a lot more to come in the next two Holiday Hits, so stay tuned!

Be sure to subscribe to my newsletter at kittythomas.com to stay aware of all the things. And thank you so much for reading and/or listening depending on what format you got the story in! (Audio is coming Summer 2024 with Jason Clarke and Meg Sylvan).

Talk to you in the next one!

Love,

Kitty ^.^

www.ingramcontent.com/pod-product-compliance
Lightning Source LLC
Chambersburg PA
CBHW032109170626
46808CB00008B/2986